The Wererat's Tale
Book III: The Collar of Perdition

THE WERERAT'S TALE, BOOK III: THE COLLAR OF PERDITION
©2021 Shane Moore

Cover art by Terry Naughton, Cover design by Frank Fradella, Edited by Edward Gehlert

A New Babel Books release
381 High Point Drive
Holiday Shores, IL 62025

www.ShaneMoorePresents.com

ISBN: 978-1-63196-034-5 (trade paperback)
Second printing.

Printed in the United States of America.

Other Abyss Walker Works

The Wererat's Tale – Book One: Of Rats and Men
The Wererat's Tale – Book Two: Ring of Nonul
White Wraith – Origins
A Walk in the Abyss
Orcs & Generals

The Abyss Walker series
The Plea of Apollisian
The Trial of Innocence
Darrion-Quieness
Death of Kings
Tides of Winter
Return of the Father

The Sword from the Sky – Patrick Tomlinson

Other Abyss Walker works
The Forge of Feasts: A Dwarven Guide to Grubbery

Other Works by Shane Moore
"I am Villian" I, Hero magazine #2
The Apocalypse of Enoch: Rapture
The Apocalypse of Enoch: Scourge
The Apocalypse of Enoch: Desolation
Lucifer: The Untold Story

1
Rat on the Run

The dark sounds of the forest were unusually quiet. The predators that stalked among the trees had become still and woods stunk of fear. Kellacun took a slow deliberate breath. She knew some of the dread was her own. Wounded and on the run from the Duke's men, her stamina was being tested like never before. She was utterly alone now, save for Kaplan. She reached down and scratched the brilliant black furred ears of the casen tiger.

Strange, Kellacun mused, that a rat's only companion should turn out to be a giant feline. She let the irony play through her mind for a moment before a snapped twig and a muffled curse returned her to the here-and-now.

"Watch it," someone whispered, "Dolan said the bitch can hear a flea fart from a hundred paces."

"Must be hard to sleep, then; that filthy rat's probably covered in them."

That's going to cost you, Kellacun thought, as a vicious smirk curled the corner of her mouth. The guard was right about one thing; even in her human form, Kellacun's senses bordered on the supernatural. Maybe even crossed over, she still didn't really understand how any of it worked. The elves certainly didn't think there was much natural about wererats, and if anyone should know, it was those tree-huggers.

She took a long, slow pull of air into her nose. There were three of them. Smells of sweat with a trace of perfume and floral notes mingled with the dirt and moss of the forest. The exotic flower smell was from a caladais, a favorite flower of one of the Duke's courtesans. The palace was filled with them at this time of year.

Kellacun grimaced. That meant these three weren't just the flunky tax-collectors and poachers she'd bested with such ease. They were drawn from the reserve of the Duke's personal guard. They would be better trained, better equipped, and the most blindly loyal. It also explained why they had continued pursuing through the night after the rest of the guards had fallen behind.

But their cushy position inside the palace had its drawbacks. The men were totally out of their element, unsupported in a dense forest in the dead of night. Their eyes would not be accustomed to such near darkness. At least they were smart enough not to carry torches.

Kellacun searched the forest floor for Kaplan, but the immense tiger's fur proved to be too good of camouflage even for her. Even though she couldn't see Kaplan, she knew what her mount was doing, maneuvering silently to find the best ambush position, then waiting to strike. She'd seen house cats play the same game with mice and ground squirrels in the alleys of Central City for years.

Kaplan was no different from them, except for the extra ton of muscle, teeth, and claws.

Kellacun stood to her full height, but winced as a fresh jolt of pain shot up through her leg. She leaned back against the tree trunk and swallowed a scream. Her leg had been broken, shattered really, in a fight with a Nonul only two days before. And even though her accelerated healing had knit the bone, her nerves still protested loudly whenever she tried to put her full weight on it.

The rest of her body wasn't fairing much better. Her swordfight with Grascon had left deep cuts and stab wounds to her back and legs, and the enchanted blade meant they would heal normally. Her demonskin armor had already mended, however, which was fortunate. It felt as though the snug armor was the only thing holding her shredded body together.

She wasn't in any condition to fight three trained killers, but her aching bones begged for rest. She needed to stop running, to sleep, and to heal. Her odds of survival shrank with every extra hour of exhaustion that piled on. Kellacun decided to take her chances and make a stand. She could count on surprise to fell her first victim, but then she'd be flanked by the two survivors. Hopefully, Kaplan would know a good opportunity when she saw it.

Kellacun decided to ramp up the men's fear by changing to her feral form. The sacrifice in finesse would be more than offset by the extra strength it afforded her, not to mention the terror it would bring out in her quarry. Panting softly, she willed her inner rat forward.

The change was... disconcerting. Her skin prickled like it was swarming with ants as thick black fur burst forth. Her elongating jaw dislocated until her nose caught up. She reset it with a click of her now chisel-like teeth. Her fingernails felt like they were being pulled out with pliers as they grew into thick, black claws. It took real effort not to scream.

Her armor stretched and morphed to fit her changing shape. A few seconds later and the painful transformation was at an end. Kellacun slowly drew the thin, enchanted blade she'd won off the first assassin the Duke had sent for her life. Her father's sabre would remain in its sheath; she wasn't sure she had the strength to wield it.

The lush forest canopy blocked nearly all moonlight from reaching the floor, so Kellacun didn't need to worry about her sword glinting and betraying her presence. Her prey was close enough now that her wild-form eyes could size up the guards individually. The man at point was the smallest, but also had the most baubles on his jerkin. The two larger men trailed behind him like loyal dogs. That answered who to take down first.

Their leader identified, Kellacun maneuvered, quiet as a temple mouse. A small, yet noisy corner of her mind still railed against the violence she was about to commit. Only a few short months ago, she had been a simple mason's daughter, blessed with loving parents and the affections of the Duke's son. That all changed late one night; the night her parents were murdered, her lover abandoned her, and the animal lurking deep inside came bursting out. It had been an incessant fight for survival and vengeance every moment since. The next few minutes would be no different.

The short man at the head of the line felt his way through the forest, one hand held out to sweep branches from his face, the other on the hilt of his sabre. Kellacun ducked behind a tree a few paces ahead of him, then pulled back a branch and held it tight. Relying on her black fur to keep her hidden, she waited until the man was only a step away, then let the branch go.

With a sharp crack, the spiny branch snapped the lead guard right in the face. He shouted out in surprise and pain. His left hand grabbed his face involuntarily, while the right fumbled to draw his sabre. He didn't get the chance. Kellacun ran out from her hiding place and grabbed the guard's wrist with her free hand, then plunged her teeth into his exposed throat. The sickening taste of hot, rusty blood exploded into her mouth. His screaming stopped abruptly as he collapsed into the leaves.

To their credit, the other two men didn't panic or run. Instead, their sabers sang pure notes as they were pulled free of their scabbards. Yet their blades cut through empty air, searching in vain for the indistinct target. One slash did manage to hit home... into one of the guard's thighs.

"Idiot! You cut me!"

"Where's Tylus?"

Kellacun's raspy, rodent voice echoed through the woods. "He's bleeding out on the ground. Leave now unless you wish to join him."

"Not likely," shouted one of the guards, "on either count." They stopped swinging pointlessly, then formed up back-to-back, sabre tips out.

Kellacun answered with a dashing attack, slashing at the wounded guard's leg, but her blade's accuracy suffered greatly from her injured back muscles. She managed only a glancing blow, shrugged off by his leather armor. His answering slash was far more effective, despite his near blindness. The sharp bite of his sword cut deeply into the gap between her chest and waist armor, but it lacked the burning Kellacun had come to associate with enchanted weapons. The wound started to heal immediately.

Buoyed with the knowledge the guards' weapons could not hurt her... much, Kellacun pressed the attack. With her light rapier, she thrust, quickly and repeatedly, trying to tire her pursuers as they defended themselves with heavier sabres. It was the same tactic Gascon had used against her only hours before, except they were nowhere near his level of swordsmanship. Neither was she, however. Her muscles burned from the effort of working around so many injuries. She knew the fight needed to be over, quickly and decisively, or her tale would end there and then.

Kellacun's ears twitched as she heard a rustling sound charging up behind her. She ducked. As if Kaplan had been listening to her thoughts, the enormous black cat dove over Kellacun's crouching body and crashed into one of the guards. Her immense weight took the man completely off his feet. Kaplan pinned him to the ground and closed her jaws around his neck and face, suffocating him.

Outnumbered by monsters, the survivor decided to drop his sword and take his chances.

"Oh, I see you can count, at least," Kellacun taunted.

"You have me, no need to rub dirt in it." His back was straight and voice tremble free. Whatever terror he felt, the guard was controlling it very well.

"What's your name?"

"Yvoni Fellax."

"Yvoni Fellax?" she repeated menacingly.

"Miss."

"That's better. A gentleman of your station must remember his manners, otherwise you'd be no better than-"

"A rat."

Kellacun lashed out with her claws, raking them across his shoulder blades. He winced, but made no sound.

"Fellax is a name of the provinces, why answer to the Duke in Central City?"

"Conscripted, miss, along with my brother, who you killed in this forest not three days ago."

Kellacun studied him for a moment, then sighed. "I have no quarrel with clan Fellax, Yvoni. You and your kin were in my way, nothing more. But here's the news, your Duke must not hold you in very high esteem, sending you out against such a dangerous opponent with weapons he knew full well couldn't do much more than irritate me."

His face twisted in confusion. "What of it?"

"I have no desire to battle with clan Fellax more than I have already. My only grief is with the Duke. He was willing to throw your life away; you have no more reason to trust him than I."

Yvoni listened intently, not that he had much choice. "And you have a proposal, I assume?"

"Yes, as a matter of fact." Kellacun reached for the dagger at the young man's side and drew it. He braced for an attack, but none came. Instead, she inspected the blade; fine craftsmanship, keen, but not enchanted. It wasn't even silver. She shook her head at Dolan's callous disregard for his own people. Then, she steeled herself and grabbed one of her thin, furry ears.

With a quick slash, Kellacun cut the ear free of her head. The pain was intense, but even more disorienting was the effect it had on her hearing. The sounds of the forest seemed to come at her from two different distances. She hoped her guess that it would grow back was right.

Apparently, Yvoni could see a little better than he'd been leading on. He jumped back in shock. "Why the hell did you do that?"

Kellacun stuffed the severed ear into the man's waistband. "So that you can go home and tell the Duke I'm dead. I have another matter to attend to, which would be easier without his assassins constantly on my tail."

Yivoni looked unconvinced, so she tried to sweeten the pot. "Think about it, Fellax, you'll be greeted as a hero. I know there's a healthy reward on my hide, enough to spend the rest of the year drunk and atop the wench of your choice."

"Everyone knows you've sworn to kill the Duke at any price. What happens to me when you come back? He'll know I lied about killing you and I'll be executed."

Kellacun pulled her lips back, revealing teeth still stained with the blood of the first guard. "Then you'll need to help me kill him before he figures it out."

Yvoni's spine stiffened to parade-ground readiness. "And if I refuse to go along with this deception and coup?"

Kellacun looked over her shoulder to where Kaplan was unabashedly gorging herself on her prey's liver. "I wasn't offering you a choice."

"I see." Yvoni weighed his non-options for a heartbeat, then looked Kellacun right in her bulging black eyes. "Looks like you have a partner."

"Excellent. Now, I must be going. I have business to the South." She turned and walked into the night, letting her human form reassert itself. Kaplan swallowed a last gulp, then trotted off after her.

"Wait! How am I supposed to get back?"

Kellacun chuckled. "You found your way in, Fellax. You can find your way back out."

* * *

Joshua paced through his room, slowly eroding a valley into the marble floor. His breakfast of poached syliban eggs and fresh cut tokur fruit sat untouched on the oak table. His eyelids pulled down heavily, but he couldn't sleep. So he paced, like a wild animal surveying the boundaries of its cage.

The door creaked open. He'd have to remind the servants to grease the hinges. His father, Duke Dolan, stepped through.

"I'm told you haven't eaten, Joshua."

Joshua glanced at the plate of cold food and smirked.

"Your spies penetrate even my bed chambers, father?"

"Of course. If only my agents were so efficient in the rest of the city. What vexes you? Still troubled by that rat girl?"

Joshua's head dipped. "I must be transparent as glass."

"Only because I know you so well, my son. What is not clear to me is the target of your frustration."

Joshua felt himself treading on thin ice indeed. His next words needed to be carefully chosen. "Kellacun, father," he paused, "and myself, I suppose."

Dolan took a seat at the table and nibbled on a piece of fruit. "You, how so?"

"Because, I was in love with her. I was preparing to ask your permission to marry her. I never suspected her true nature. How could my judgment have been so blind?"

Dolan just chuckled. "You suffer the same affliction as all healthy young men, my boy. Nothing kills a man's reason faster than fluttering eyelashes and rosy lips. The weapons women wield are softer than our own, but just

as deadly. Never forget that."

Joshua nodded. "I won't." He walked over to the ceremonial arsenal hanging on his wall. He made a show of perusing the selection of blades, maces, and shields before pulling a thin silver dagger from its sheath. "In

fact, I'd like to turn that very weapon on its owner."

Dolan's eyebrow twitched. "What are you proposing?"

"Think, father. Every assassin you've sent after Kellacun has returned in a box, or several. That thieving rat Pavco and his pathetic 'guild' have failed as well, possibly by design."

"And you believe you can succeed where they have failed?"

"Yes, absolutely."

Dolan shook his head. "I'm afraid not, Joshua, I won't risk my only heir. That bitch hasn't just killed my best men, she's slaughtered them like cattle. You've grown into a fine swordsman, but you don't have the experience of your masters. One of whom fell to Kellacun's blades, I would remind you."

"But that's the beauty of it, father. I won't have to fight her. She wants you dead, not me. You saw it with your own eyes last night. She wouldn't fight me, even as I tried to plunge my blade into her heart."

"And then you promised to kill her. An oath she is unlikely to forget, Joshua."

"I'll say it was out of anger, in the panic to protect you."

Dolan's face became solemn as he weighed the proposal.

"I can do this, Father. Let me prove my worth with this errand."

"Do you really believe you have the fortitude to kill your first love?"

"You misjudge me. My family and this castle are my first love. The lust I once felt for Kellacun pales in comparison."

The Duke smiled. "Well played, my boy. Very well, you have my permission to undertake this mission. Indeed, it will be your first official assignment."

"I will not fail, father."

"I'm sure of it, Joshua. But be wary. Central City will need a new Duke one day, and I don't want to start another one from scratch."

2
River Rats

Days in the forest started to merge together. The thick canopy of leaves and intertwining branches kept the ground in a near perpetual dusk as it was, making it difficult for Kellacun to get a sense of the time. Night fell with alarming suddenness, and carried its own dangers. A bear had taken a strong interest in her on the second night, or more specifically, the meat on her bones. But a brief stare-down and some growling with Kaplan convinced him it wouldn't be worth the fight.

They had been walking through the forest for almost a week. Kellacun could scarcely believe how far it extended. Trails interrupted here and there, and the occasional clearing gave her just enough sky to confirm that they were still headed south. Despite proving to be a much better hunter of men than game, Kellacun ate well. Kaplan's skills more than made up for her shortcomings, and she was surprisingly eager to share her kills. Kellacun couldn't help but feel a bit like the tiger was treating her like an oddly-shaped cub.

Still, the forest's size and density were its greatest assets for Kellacun at the moment, despite the slow going. Her new friend Fellax should have reached Central City by now and reported her "death" to Duke Dolan, provided he hadn't met a bear of his own. It was her job now to keep from creating any rumors of her escape until they were well beyond the reach of the duke's spies and contacts. The further she traveled undetected, the safer she would be.

She realized that her hand had absently started rubbing at her missing ear. A bud of a new lobe had started to grow in, but it was still small and itched terribly. Apparently replacing whole body parts was a steeper hill to climb than just repairing damaged ones, even for her enhanced healing powers. Fortunately, Kaplan's were the only eyes around to see her disfigurement.

Kellacun struggled yet again to keep despair at bay. Her wild form aside, she was not a creature of the outdoors. Until a few short months ago, her entire life had passed by ensconced in the protective, if dirty, confines of Central City's barrier walls. The forest's sounds and odors were as alien to her as she had been to the elves. But as little as she knew about the forest, she knew less still about where she was headed.

The Kingdom of Nalir lay so far to the south that Kellacun had only met a handful of traders that hailed from it. They were a rough-and-tumble bunch, but she supposed a month's travel over river and road had more than a little to do with their temperaments by the time they reached Central City's gates. Of their King, Hector, she knew nothing at all, except that Grascon believed she could find work with him. Any King that would employ a foreign wererat assassin was probably a shady enough character to be wary of in the first place. She chuckled at the thought.

Kaplan's ears perked up suddenly. She let out a low, challenging grumble a moment before Kellacun's good ear picked up the intruder. Her enchanted rapier was drawn in a flash as she spun to face the unannounced newcomer. As quickly as she'd brought the tip to bear, she dropped it again.

"What do *you* want?" The question came out in a heavy sigh.

"Good to see you again as well, wererat," replied the centaur.

"Caballus, wasn't it?"

The horseman nodded.

"You made it plain when we met how you felt about my... people."

Arms as thick as Kellacun's thighs crossed over Caballus's chest. "That was before you fought against those sewer rats from the city, defending my elf friends in the cave."

Kellacun snorted as she sheathed her rapier. "Fat lot of good my help did them, considering I was the only survivor."

"Still, you tried, which is more than I can say for some of us in the woods."

He sounded troubled, almost wistful. Not something Kellacun would have expected from a fey. "You wanted
to stand with the elves?" He nodded.

"Well then why didn't you?"

His smile conveyed anything but happiness. "Fey are not nearly as independent as you might think. There
are traditions to follow."

"You know what my father used to say about traditions?"

Caballus shook his head.

"Traditions are what we call things when nobody can remember why we keep doing them."

Caballus craned his head back and let out a belly laugh that shook the trees to their roots. "Your father is a clever one, I think."

A fresh pang of guilt and anger shot through Kellacun's stomach. "Yes, he was."

The centaur's mood dimmed in response to her pain. He looked for a moment as though he would offer comfort, but thought better of it. "At any rate, I felt compelled to repay the blood you shed for my friends, even if the gesture is only a token." He reached a big, calloused hand into a knapsack strapped to his horsebody. It reemerged holding a familiar-looking shape swathed in linen.

He slowly unwrapped the cloth, revealing her missing trophy. "I believe you dropped this."

Kellacun surged forward, gently taking the offered blade from Caballus's hands. "How did you get this? Quasias still had it with him when, ah…"

"When something turned him into foie gras?" Caballus smirked. "Yes, I'd be interested to know how you did that."

"I'm afraid there won't be a repeat of that performance."

"Pity, the forest has some pests that could use clearing out. Listen, you've earned that blade twice now; once when you took it from the Al-Kalidian, and again when you killed the birdman. Try to keep a better hold of it, though."

Kellacun slid the thin rapier into its waiting sheath. "Thank you."

"None needed. Our debts cancel now, wererat. You're nearing the forest's edge. By the end of the day, you'll reach the river. If you hurry, you can catch a ride with a bargeman named Steyer. He can take you south much faster."

"Thanks, but I doubt anyone's going to give passage to a girl and her giant tiger."

"Steyer won't mind, he's blind."

Kellacun snorted. "Blind, maybe, but surely he can still hear and smell."

Caballus winked conspiratorially. "Plausible deniability."

"Ah, I see. ...Caballus?"

The centaur raised an eyebrow, prodding her to continue.

"There will always be someone to carry on tradition. If there's something you believe is worth fighting for, maybe you should be the one fighting."

The horseman stamped a hoof nervously, unsure of what to say.

"Surely you're not afraid?" Kellacun asked incredulously. "Look at you, you could be your own calvary charge!"

Caballus stroked his short beard thoughtfully. "Hmm, I suppose I could at that. Hardly seems fair, does it?"

"Fighting seldom is. Good day, my... acquaintance."

The horseman smiled thinly, then cupped a hand beside his mouth to whisper. "You may call me friend, Kellacun. Just not too loudly."

"Understood. Be well."

The centaur gave a small bow, then turned back into the forest and disappeared as suddenly as he'd came. Kellacun rubbed the pommel of her reclaimed sword, scratched Kaplan behind the ear, then continued south.

The fey's advice proved useful. Kellacun pressed on through the thinning forest, emerging on the banks of the Dawson River just in time to catch Steyer casting off his lines. She somehow managed to convince Kaplan to remain concealed in the bushes, despite the language barrier between them. The cat was proving to be very cunning. Kellacun wasn't sure if she should feel relieved or concerned.

She waved a hand at the bargeman to get his attention, then slapped herself on the forehead when she remembered the man was blind.

"Hail Steyer!" she called out.

On the deck of his barge, the man turned an ear towards the unfamiliar voice. "Who calls for me?" he shouted in reply.

Kellacun walked down the sandy bank towards the barge. It seemed to be little more than a couple dozen empty whiskey barrels lashed to planks that formed the deck. Still, it appeared solid enough for her purposes.

"I was sent by Caballus, he said you're known to take on passengers."

"I am. What's your name, young lady?"

"He also said you weren't one to ask too many questions," she said as sweetly as possible.

"Ah, I see. One of those stories. Well lass, in that case I have only two questions; how much weight, and how do you plan to pay?"

The tension left Kellacun's shoulders. "It's just me and my, um, horse. So call it eighty stone. And I have silver."

Steyer held out a wrinkled hand shaped by decades spent pulling rope. Kellacun dropped a pair of coins into his palm. He held them up to his ear and klinked them together, then touched them to his tongue. "Fine, fine. How far are you going?"

"Nalir."

"End of the line, huh? I'll need two more of these." He rubbed the coins together.

"And you shall have them when we reach Nalir."

His eyes continued staring over her shoulder, but creases appeared on his forehead. "Trying to dupe poor

blind Steyer, are you girl?"

"No, sir," Kellacun shook her head, "my coin purse grows light is all. I must be sure I get what I pay for." Steyer's weatherworn face softened. "Okay, lass, hold onto your money. I don't mind earning my keep. Better bring your horse aboard, I'm ready to sail."

"Thank you." Kellacun turned and waved a hand to her mount in the bushes. Once again interpreting her intentions correctly, Kaplan stood and slinked towards the river bank. Kellacun wasn't sure how the giant cat was going to feel about being in the middle of so much water.

Steyer cast off the last of his lines, then bent over to grab a pair of long, thick boards. Years moving cargo had given him a strong back, and he hefted both of them with ease. "Give me a hand with these."

"Where do they go?"

"They're ramps, girl, for your-" Steyer was interrupted by the sudden impact of Kaplan's immense weight landing on the far side of the deck. Steyer and Kellacun fought to stay afoot under the pitching barge. "-horse?"

"Sorry," Kellacun purred, "she fancies herself a jumper."

"Uh-huh. Funny shoes you have on her, too. Most hooves go, 'clop-clop.'"

"Well…"

Steyer put up a hand. "I don't care, miss. Just keep whatever it is from eating me and we can stay friends, okay?"

"Okay," Kellacun replied somewhat sheepishly.

"Get your 'horse' to stay in the middle of the barge, and don't let it move around too much." Steyer stuck a pole into the muddy bank and pushed off. "And keep it away from my lamb jerky!"

The barge sailed south through the night. With her eyes fully adjusted to the sliver of light from the moon, Kellacun stood on the prow and watched the land drift by. Every moment that passed took her further away from what had once been her home than she had ever traveled. But further from what? Further from the bodies of her parents? Further from Joshua and their dead love? Further from the den of thieves and assassins paid to slaughter her?

Maybe further was better after all, she decided. The river was quiet, with only the shuffling sound of Steyer's sandals as he moved down the length of the barge with his pole. There was little traffic on the Dawson at this hour. Most every boat, barge, and canoe had pulled ashore until morning returned. Of course, the dark provided little challenge for a blind pilot.

"You are still awake, miss?"

"Yes, I'm a bit of a night owl."

"I'm not, I've been trolling this creek since before you were born. Still struggle to keep awake some nights."

Kellacun's forehead rumpled with questions. She picked one at random to start with. "How do you know how old I am?"

What? A blind man can't hear the silky sound of a youthful voice? Or the smell of a girl just coming into womanhood? Or the..." He breathed in through his nose, carefully sampling confusing odors. "Or a horse that smells suspiciously like a pile of wet barn cats."

"Um..."

"I said I didn't care."

"Thank you."

"It's better for both of us."

"Okay, but why not just work during the day?"

Steyer snorted a laugh. "Ironically, because there were too many 'captains' with perfectly good eyes who couldn't find the time to use them. I got tired of replacing barrels every time a distracted boat blundered into me. The worst part was I almost always had to pay for the damage to both boats. Everyone knew the accidents

must have been the blind man's fault."

"I'm sorry. That's terrible."

"Don't worry, lass. I may grumble, but my new schedule has opened up new... business opportunities for me. Passengers like yourself, who prefer to move unseen."

Kellacun couldn't help but smirk. "You're perfect for the job, my friend. I'm sure you have stories to tell."

"No, I don't, which is what you paid for."

"Of course."

Steyer turned his head and listened to the frogs as they chirped the night away, ever optimistic in love.

"I have learned one thing that I can share freely."

"I'd be grateful."

"The river makes running easy. The current carries you from whatever troubles you, fast and far. Problem is, there always comes a time to stop running. And the further away the river takes you, the harder the journey home will be."

"I understand, but I'm not running. I'm here to keep a promise."

"Promises are easy to come by in Nalir, but hard to keep."

"Okay, do you have practical wisdom in addition to the folksy, sage advice?"

Steyer smirked. "I might. What do you want to know?"

"How well do you know Nalir and her King?"

"King Hector is an impressive man. Then again, one would have to be to beat Nalir's festering swamps into a functioning kingdom, even if only just. He is ambitious, cunning, and ruthless. Be wary of that one."

"I thought you said he was a good man?"

"I said he was an *impressive* man, that doesn't mean *good*. Often it means precisely the opposite. Hector is not needlessly cruel; he does not relish inflicting suffering as some tyrants do, but neither does he scrupulously avoid it. Whatever vision he holds for Nalir's future, it's his first priority. His people are tools to further that vision, nothing more."

"What of a merc called Bladewright? Do you know anything about him?"

"That old half-blood? Stay clear of him."

"Half-blood? What do you mean?"

"He's half-orc, and a dangerous one at that."

Kellacun unconsciously rested a palm on the pommel of her saber. "What makes him so dangerous?"

"Being tainted with orc blood will make anyone twitchy, but he embraced his violent heritage. He was a fearsome warrior for many years, but now he's a warrior without a war. He turned to drink to quell his demons."

"Great," Kellacun sighed, "another drunk."

"A drunk? Heavens no, lass. Drunks are sloppy amateurs. He's elevated it to an art form." Steyer pointed to the barrels that kept his barge afloat. "Personally witnessed him drain one o' these whisky barrels in one evening, then gift it to me to repair my boat."

"Well that was... nice of him."

"Oh aye, he can be very friendly, but his mood changes quicker than a mountain wind. And you never can tell what's going to flip the lever."

Kellacun had no more questions for him, and Steyer fell silent. The barge drifted down the river guided by only an occasional nudge of Steyer's pole against the steep banks. Kellacun wondered at how he could tell when the boat was coming too close, so she closed her eyes. She felt the boat rolling gently against the waves and ripples, listened to the trickling of the water against the barrels. Her ear still itched, but had grown back to nearly full size and no longer impeded her hearing. The calls of frogs and crickets merged into a harmony of notes until one was almost indistinguishable from the other.

The calls ebbed, then died away entirely on the nearby stretch of beach. On cue, Steyer pushed his pole against the river bed, casting the barge back into the current. So simple, yet so easy to overlook. Kellacun resolved to spend more time honing all of her new senses.

It had been a long, difficult few days. For the first time since her failed attempt on the Duke's life, she felt at relative ease. There were no dangers on the raft, and those who had been pursuing her drifted further away with each league. Content with her unexpected security, Kellacun nestled up against Kaplan's soft black fur. The tiger couldn't purr, but she let out a satisfied sigh and extended a heavy, protective paw over her friend's chest. Warmed by the cat's body heat, Kellacun sank into a deep, dreamless sleep.

Kellacun felt something probing her side. Her eyes snapped open, but were blinded by a sudden flash of sunlight. She lashed with one hand, finding an arm touching her ribs, while long, black claws grew reflexively from her other hand in preparation.

"Easy, girl. It's time to wake up. We're in Nalir."

The voice was Steyer's. She had slept straight through the rest of the night and well into the morning. Her eyes adjusted quickly to see the bargeman leaning over her, offering a hand to help her up. She accepted.

"What time is it?"

"Sorry, that's one thing I'm not brilliant at."

Kellacun chuckled softly. "I suppose not. Thank you for the lift." She reached into her purse and turned over a pair of silver coins. "The balance of my fare, as promised."

"Much obliged, miss."

Steyer held up his hands. "I never even saw you," he said with a mischievous grin.

"Right." Kellacun gathered herself up. Kaplan yawned, and stretched out her legs in a decadent display of feline laziness. With considerable effort, she raised herself up from the deck and slunk off towards the pier.

A pair of dock workers extended a rickety boarding ramp to meet the barge. To their credit, they only paused for a heartbeat at the sight of Kaplan siting on her haunches. Obviously, stranger things than a pretty girl and her giant cat had come through Nalir. Kellacun helped Steyer tie off his mooring lines before walking down the plank herself. She turned to wave at the bargeman, then slapped herself a second time. "Smooth sailing, Steyer!"

The old sailor turned and faced the sound of her voice. "When you're ready for the long trip home, look me up. Oh, and you might find what you're looking for at the Bog Water tavern."

"Thanks!" Kellacun spun around on a heel and started down the pier.

The Dawson River had widened into a vast delta plain, rife with sandbars and mangroves. The odorous swamps of Nalir spread before her, crisscrossed with a web of timber dykes and earthen levies. Roads made of roughly hewn stone sat atop the wider, taller levies. In the distance, a hill clawed for the sky. It was the only feature on the horizon. A road spiraled its way around the hill, before reaching an enormous walled keep, perched atop the hill like a stone crown. Built up around the base was a ramshackle ring of buildings. If one was feeling generous, it could even be called a city.

Wagons carrying trade goods from the port streamed towards the city, while carts carrying mud from the swamps streamed towards the river's edge. The buildings surrounding the port seemed limited to warehouses, trader's stalls, and stables. Kellacun was confident the Bog Water wouldn't be found here. She got the attention of one of the more... colorful-looking dock workers. It wasn't difficult; he was already staring at her.

"Good morning," she said cheerfully. "I'm looking for-"

"Don't say a stable." The dockman pointed a gnarled finger at Kaplan. "Ain't nobody going to board *that* thing."

"I was actually going to ask about a tavern, the Bog Water? Do you know where I can find it?"

"The lady likes to live dangerously."

Kellacun stroked the black fur of Kaplan's neck. "Wouldn't you if you had pets like her?"

"Ha! I might at that, girl." He jabbed a thumb towards the ring city surrounding the hilltop castle. "It's on the far side, corner of Determination and Perseverance."

Kellacun cocked an eyebrow. "Strange names for streets."

"Hector's idea. S'posed to remind us little people of our morals."

"How's that working?"

"Hasn't taken root with me, but mum always said my head wasn't very fertile ground."

Kellacun smirked. "Thanks, I'll let you back to work." The laborer tipped his cap and returned to coiling rope. Kellacun turned to the hill, which she estimated to be several miles distant. She looked at Kaplan and toyed with the idea of taking a ride, but decided against it. Her wounds were close to healed, and the day spent languishing on Steyer's barge had left her legs and hips stiff. A brisk walk would do them good.

3
The Swamps of Nalir

It was Dolan's turn to pace. The floor of his throne room was clad in an intricate pattern of creamy marble and red granite, with silver trim between the joints. It had not come cheaply, and had required the labors of a dozen masons for nearly a month. Masons Dolan had executed soon thereafter when it was discovered they did not harbor the best of intentions for the Duke's continued rule.

He'd watched the day before as Joshua, his only son and heir, had saddled up the fastest horse in the Duke's stables and departed on his first assignment outside Central City's walls. An assignment, Dolan learned this morning, that may have been entirely in vain, but there was no way to tell Joshua that now.

Dolan made a note from now on only to lend operatives his *second* fastest horse.

The door creaked open and Vical, Dolan's Chief of Staff, poked his head through. "Sire, the, um, 'leader' of the Thieves Guild has arrived as you requested."

"Show him in, Vical."

"Very good, sir. Will you require refreshments?"

"Oh, I don't think we need to waste good wine on the likes of him."

"As you wish." Vical's head withdrew. A moment later, the door swung open and disgorged the portly, disheveled form of Pavco into Dolan's presence. It was obvious that both men would be much happier once the encounter had concluded.

Dolan nodded to his guest. "Pavco."

"Your grace," the wererat thief said sarcastically. "Don't worry about the wine; I have better stock at home."

"I'm sure." Dolan motioned for his guest to have a seat in an elegantly carved high-back chair. "And more comfortable furniture, no doubt."

Pavco let his girth fall into the chair. Wooden legs creaked under the unexpected burden. "Eh, not really. The rats tend to steal all the stuffing for nesting. Difficult little buggers to eradicate." His face twisted into a proud grin. His meaning was not lost on Dolan, but he was being clever beyond his capacities. The thief was overconfident in his strength, but that was fine with the duke. Overconfident adversaries made mistakes. All a smart man need do was keep out their way and wait.

"Funny you should say that, because our rodent problem is exactly what I called you here to discuss."

"I told you already, she's gone. Deep into the forest with that tiger she found. And Grascon's disappeared too. His head is suddenly very valuable because of that little stunt."

"It continues to amaze me how much trouble an entire den of wererat thieves has killing one little wererat girl. Aren't thieves supposed to be good at finding things that are well hidden?"

"Don't question my dedication, Dolan. I lost over a dozen men to that bitch during the forest raid. 'sides, it's not like you've done much better. How many guards of yours has she scrapped? Not to mention that giant iron toy you handed her."

Dolan held up a hand. "That's enough. We can agree that Kellacun has been a most persistent thorn in both of our sides, but that may have changed. As it happens, she was found in the deep of the forest by three of my personal reserve guards."

"Really? Who found *their* bodies?"

"No one," Dolan said as he walked for the door. He opened it a crack and whispered to Vical, "Send him in."

Dolan withdrew as another man dressed in the uniform of the Duke's Reserve entered the throne room. He was medium height, powerfully built, yet walked with a pronounced limp.

"Pavco, may I introduce Yvoni Fellax, fresh from an excursion to the forest. He has an interesting story to tell us."

* * *

The fetid plains of Nalir were deceptively broad. Kellacun and Kaplan had been walking for well over an hour and seemed only marginally closer to the ring city. The levy they tread upon ran parallel to a row of windmills bigger than any she'd ever seen.

On a ridgeline outside Central City, she'd seen smaller machines capture the wind to turn mill stones and grind wheat and corn. Here in Nalir, however, they turned giant screw-tubes, sucking the swamps dry of water and spilling it over the tops of the dykes and back into the sea.

Once drained, each walled plot of land was left with a thick layer of incredibly fertile muddy soil. These were then turned to agriculture. Kellacun had seen rice, barley, beats, potatoes, lithurgal beans, even grape vines growing in the reclaimed land.

The miles rolled past into the afternoon. Every half mile or so, a set of flood gates were cut into the dyke. The gates angled inwards, propped up from beneath with thick timbers. Strangely, the timbers were cut straight through the middle, with large chains secured below the cuts. It took Kellacun several minutes to puzzle out the purpose of the strange arrangement. With a jerk of the chains, the timbers would buckle and collapse, dropping the gate and letting the ocean flood the land once more. It was only then that she noticed the road she and Kaplan walked on actually sat below the dykes.

Any army intent on invading Nalir would quickly find themselves drowned by the sea. The castle hill would effectively be turned into an island, requiring a navy to lay siege to it. The entire kingdom had been designed from the ground up to be a booby trap. Steyer had been right; King Hector was an impressive man indeed.

The city grew closer, and the smells of swamp, livestock, and agriculture began to mingle with the scents of smith shops, fermentation, tanning, and the great unwashed masses inside Kellacun's nose. Tendrils of grey and black smoke rose from a hundred different chimneys, clouding a clear view of the approach to the castle at the hill's summit.

Kellacun stepped ahead of Kaplan as they approached a check point of sorts. The ring city presented no wall, mote, or other obvious defenses. Instead, a wooden gate straddled the road's stones. A small, rickety sentry hut stood to one side, while an equally rickety sentry manned the gate.

"Halt!" called out a voice that sounded like the winds of time themselves. The ancient sentry was armed with only a short spear, which pulled double-duty as a cane.

Kellacun stopped as instructed and waited politely for the old man to shuffle around the barricade. He drew himself up to his full height, which was still a handspan shorter than Kellacun. "What brings you to Nalir, young lady?"

"Business," Kellacun replied, "of a private nature."

"How long will you be staying with us?"

"I'm not sure yet, but perhaps for a while."

"Very well, but your, ah, friend there will need to stay outside the city."

Kellacun had been afraid something like this was coming. "Are you sure that's a good idea? You have an awful lot of sheep and cattle wandering around out here."

"Better missing lambs than missing people, young miss."

She was about to object, until remembering the fallen guard in the forest, and the unsettling look of contentment on Kaplan's face as she dined on him. "You may have a point, there."

"We have quite a feral pig problem in the fields, there's even a bounty. Perhaps your friend can be put to good use."

Kellacun scratched the tiger behind an ear. "What do you think, Kaplan? Can you stick to pork for a few days?" The cat chuffed happily. Whether it was in understanding or just appreciation of a good scratch, Kellacun couldn't say. "All right, I'm trusting you. No two-legged meals, agreed?"

Kaplan regarded her with a pained expression, then plopped down on her haunches. With that sorted, the frail sentry swung open the timber gate, allowing Kellacun to sweep past.

"Enjoy your stay," he called to her back.

Once past the gate, the familiar sights and sounds of the city surrounded Kellacun. Unlike the crowded, chaotic streets of Central City, though, Nalir's ring was new and organized. The very oldest structures had been built less than a generation ago. The broad streets were arranged in an orderly grid of concentric circles and radiating lines. The city's youth and order did little to advance cleanliness, however. Building materials consisted mainly of fired bricks made of clay and manure, which left the city with a... uniquely earthy odor.

Evidence abound in gutters running to either side of the streets that the city lacked the network of sewer tunnels Kellacun and the Thieves Guild had come to rely on back home. But of course it would, she realized. The water level must be only a few inches below the surface. There would be nowhere for sewers to run to.

She found Determination Street two rings in, after Strength and Unity, and followed it to the right. If the dockworker's word proved reliable, Bog Water would be on the opposite side of the castle hill anyway. She studied the castle as she continued. It was made of stacked stone, roughly hewn, but no less effective for its crudeness. Unless the builders had completely cannibalized a nearby hill, the stone must have come from far up river, and at great expense.

The hill itself had also been worked. A slowly spiraling road led from the base all the way to the castle at the top, completing a total of seven revolutions as it did so. At first, Kellacun thought it wasteful, as a short series of switchbacks could have achieved the same and reduced the time carts took to reach the summit. But then she remembered the floodgates on the plains. The spiraling road was yet another defense. Invaders would have to march all the way around the hill seven times, all the while being inundated with arrows, crossbow bolts, rocks, burning oil, and whatever else the besieged defenders had stockpiled in there. Building a ramp would prove difficult, considering the hill would be surrounded by a shallow sea.

Kellacun began to wonder what sort of a man would go to such extreme lengths to defend himself from attack.

In the final tally, Nalir was still mostly just a swamp. The planning of the kingdom and keep bordered on a sort of engineering paranoia. What exactly was King Hector afraid of. Or, an even more worrisome possibility, what was he hiding?

The time for idle speculation was over as she reached Perseverance Street. Sure enough, on the corner sat, slouched really, a building claiming the mantle of Bog Water. Age hadn't yet had time to account for the structure's unhealthy slant, which was instead owed simply to sloppy craftsmanship. Standing outside the door were several patrons who stood just as straight as the bar they'd just exited, despite it being mid-afternoon. One of them busied himself redistributing his share of ale into the gutter.

Kellacun's eyes rolled back far enough to see the roots of her hair. *Why does it always have to be the most disreputable, unstable looking tavern in the city,* she thought. *Surely there's a nice art museum somewhere? Maybe a sports arena?*

Annoyed, yet undeterred, she walked straight and true for the bar. The shudder-style door swung inward at her push. Pipe-smoke stained windows allowed little light to enter along with her, but judging by the shabby state of the occupants, that was probably a good thing on balance. Her eyes adjusted quickly, and Kellacun scanned the room for her quarry. It didn't take long to find him.

Sitting at a table in the corner, loudly regaling an audience of empty whiskey bottles, sat the single ugliest man Kellacun had ever laid eyes on. Every adjacent table was empty. She pushed past several gawking onlookers and came to a stop in front of the half-blood.

"I'm looking for a man named Bladewright. You him?"

The lump of man stopped in mid-sentence and turned his face to consider her. Short tusks protruded from his lower jaw, leaving a convenient path for a thin line of drool. "Exchuse me, madam, but I wassin the middle of a story."

"Story time's over. I'm looking for work."

Bladewright tipped his chair back on two legs and smiled crookedly. "Oh really? Well then, little lady, you can go to work clearing out my empty friends here and getting me fresh ones." He took in a deep breath in preparation for a hearty laugh, but Kellacun didn't offer him the chance. She snapped a foot out hard, cracking one of the chair legs and sending the half-orc tumbling backwards into the wall. He rolled with the collapse and thrust his boots against the floor trim. His feet planted, he launched himself towards Kellacun like a stone from a catapult. Shocked at his reflexes, Kellacun barely ducked the attack in time to watch him sail overhead, then she rolled under the table and kicked it over, putting a two-inch thick oak barricade between them.

Standing fast, Kellacun drew both of her enchanted rapiers as Bladewright regained his footing. The bar fell dead silent, until only the pure tone of her still-ringing swords filled the air. Everyone in the room stared. Not at her, not at the half-orc, but at the silver blades in her hands. Several palms gripped the pommels of their own swords and daggers, while intent eyes watched for her next move.

Bladewright broke the silence. "You have a lot of nerve coming into Nalir brandishing Al'Kalidian steel. Where'd you get those swords, girl? You elf kin?"

"Not likely. These are trophies, from the first assassins I killed. The *first*, not the *last*."

Bladewright's eyes narrowed. His stance was solid, betraying no trace of the many bottles of whiskey he'd drained. "I'd call you a liar and have these men kill you, if you didn't move so damned fast. How do you know my name?"

"A mutual friend told me I might find an old, wore-out merc down here who might get me noticed with Hector."

"That's right fancy, girl. This 'friend' got a name?"

"Not that I recall, but he did say 'Long live the Undaunted.'"

"Well," Bladewright smirked. "That shortens the list rather considerably. Turn that table right and grab a chair. Let's talk business."

The hands in the bar left their pommels and returned to their tankards as Kellacun sheathed her swords. She pushed the table back over as Bladewright sat down. "So, you're looking for merc work? Why should I hire you?"

"Because I've killed a pair of Al'Kalidian assassins after my scalp. That should be enough resume for anybody. Better question is why should I work for you?" Bladewright apparently found this very amusing.

"What's so funny?" Kellacun demanded.

"I'm just trying to figure out if your bravado comes from an excess of bravery, or for want of brains." He swiped a fresh whiskey bottle from the clammy hand of the barkeep and ripped out the cork with his teeth. "Our friend didn't share many stories with you, I see. If he did, you wouldn't have to ask about my qualifications.

These elves you killed, what were they wearing?"

"I... um..."

"What, don't remember? Let me save you some time.

They were wearing black capes with silver trim, right?"

"How do you know that?"

"Because your accent is from up river, pretty far. I'd guess you're from Central City or thereabouts. Al'Kalidians wandering that far north are only going to

come from one cast. The black cast is real, bottom of
the barrel scum. They're the lowest knot on the
Al'Kalidian rope. They usually get fed up with being
treated like dogs after a hundred years or so and strike
out on their own as sell-swords, trading on the
fearsome reputation of the Al'Kalidian name with
people who don't know any better.

"So, yeah, you killed a couple dregs, which was no
small feat I'm sure. But don't confuse them with actual
Al'Kalidians. Hell, the real elves would probably thank
you for your trouble before killing you to take back
their steel. You may be tough enough for Central City,
but face it, you're out of your element here. Which
makes you a risk for a business-minded man such as
myself."

Kellacun had to work to maintain a proper facade of
indignant affrontery, but she knew Bladewright had
struck an accurate blow. She knew nothing of this city,
the kingdom, or its people. She hadn't spared a
thought of what drawing Al'Kalidian swords would
mean to the locals. At least she knew what dangers
waited for her back home, but here, she could be killed
without a moment's notice, and without ever knowing
why.

Not that she was going to let that stop her.

"I admit that I'm new here, but I'm not new to the
job, and I learn quickly. I have… unique skills to offer."

The half-orc snorted. "I've sailed with an albino
Minotaur. How 'unique' can you be?"

Kellacun narrowed her gaze and let her voice drop
to a whisper. "Pray you never have to find out."

Bladewright shook his head and took a long, slow
pull of whiskey. Once the burning liquid had run its

course into his stomach, he leveled his yellow eyes at Kellacun like a pair of javelins. "Tell you what, I'm going to hire you. If you're as good as you boast, you'll be a good investment. If you're just bluffing me, your death will be very satisfying. Either way, I come out ahead."

"Sounds fair," Kellacun said with far more confidence than she felt. "What's the job?"

"There's no reason for you to know, but we have a very serious hog problem out on the plains."

Kellacun nodded. "I've heard as much, wild pigs are wrecking the crops, so what?"

"Ahh, you've heard of the piglets, not the sow. The momma pig is a monster, and she needs killin'. Oh, and one crack about it being a relative of mine and I'll split your skull right here."

"Wouldn't dream of it," Kellacun lied smoothly. "But it's just a pig, there has to be someone in the castle who can kill it?"

"Three volunteers thought so, too. All we found were their boots. This isn't just a slab of bacon, the sow weighs over fifty stone. Hector is tired of wasting good men on her, so he asked me to find some poor sap to do
the job. You're the sap of the day."

Kellacun ignored the jab. "How much coin?"

"No coin. Think of this as an audition."

"No coin? I have to eat!"

"Well if you succeed, you'll get fifty stone of pork, ham, and bacon. That should keep a skinny little waif like you fed for months."

Kellacun crossed her arms. "That's not funny."

"Why? You're not one of those meatless, grass-eating weirdoes, are you?"

"No, I'm one of those 'weirdoes' who likes to get paid for their work."

"Coin's not all you want. You want an audience with King Hector. That only happens if I sign off on your metal. You want to prove you're good enough? This is how you're going to do it. So, what's it going to be, sister?"

* * *

"What do you think of Mr. Fellax's story?" Dolan laced his fingers together and leaned back in his chair.

Pavco picked a fingernail. "I think he's either an incredibly brave soldier, or an incredibly brave liar."

"There is great risk of death in either case, that is true. But of the particulars, do they hold up to what you know of your… people?"

"Mostly. The only way I've seen, without silver or enchanted weapons of course, to truly kill a 'rat is to cut off their head. I suppose braining one with a big enough rock would probably do the same job. Makes one wonder, though."

"Wonder what, exactly?"

"How a man who can barely walk can get close enough to a 'rat to hit her with a damned rock. Especially *that* 'rat."

"Yes, but keep in mind that Kellacun was wounded. Your man Grascon did accomplish that much.

"True, I s'pose. Still, awful convenient that he was the only survivor. No one else to counter his story."

"And convenient that he destroyed her head, making it useless for identification purposes," Dolan added.

"*And* that he was too wounded to drag the body back out with him, but not so badly that he couldn't get back to the city himself."

Dolan sat in contemplation for several long moments.

"What of the ear, then?"

"See," Pavco settled deeper into his chair, "that's the one thing I can't ignore. It's a 'rat ear, no mistake, and the dry blood on his dagger also matched. It's not like she'd have just let him saunter up and cut off a trophy, is it?"

"That would seem, improbable, yes." Dolan scratched at his goatee. "So you believe Mr. Fellax?"

"Not as far as I can piss pudding. She may have cut it off herself to try and trick us. If that's the case, he's working with the bitch. I'd kill him first chance, if it were me."

The duke couldn't help but smile. "While such tactics may work among criminals, Pavco, in polite society it is considered bad form to execute people for doing their jobs well. The rest of my guards are already hailing him a hero. Killing him now would not help palace morale."

Pavco waved a chubby arm dismissively. "Naw, you've got it all wrong. Don't scrap him right away. Pay him his bounty, let him run around town for a couple months, drinking and whoring to his heart's content, then when everybody's forgotten about it, he can die accidentally, see? Maybe even have one of my boys do it, then Mr. Fellax can die bravely in the line of duty, the public gets its hero's funeral, and you are out a potential assassin."

Dolan smiled thinly. "I'm impressed, Pavco, you're starting to think like a noble. Consider it a contract, then. Mr. Fellax will have a very happy, very short, rest of his life."

"Fine, fine. What about Kellacun? How can we be sure she's dead?"

"Simple, my dear thief, we wait. If she hasn't come after me again in the next few months, it's because she's feeding beetles."

4
Hunting for Ham

Kellacun's boot sunk halfway to her knee into the stagnant, brown water of the bog. It oozed over the top of the boot's leather, soaking her foot in the warm, sickly liquid.

"Wonderful." She tried to pull her leg back out, but the muck seemed to constrict, holding her foot fast. Annoyance and a sprinkle of panic took hold, and she jerked up with all of the enhanced strength her 'gift' had bestowed. Mercifully, her foot came free, and for a moment Kellacun smiled in triumph. Until she realized she was staring at her toes. Her boot remained mired in the morass.

"Naturally!" she groaned as she grabbed the boot and gave it a tug. But it was hopeless. She decided it was probably ruined and took off the other one, then tossed it in the mud. She'd never liked those boots anyway, they didn't fit her right. And as long as she was telling herself comforting lies, she would soon have enough coin to have custom boots cobbled from the most expensive and durable leather.

She stood and started down the 'trail' again. Her bare feet moved much more easily over the soggy earth, and it wasn't long before she was glad to be rid of the boots. The trail she was following was little more than a line of wooden planks that had been laid down in the swamp. Reeds and cattails had grown up around the planks, giving passersby some limited footing.

Kaplan strut proudly ahead of her. Despite the cat's immense size, her four large paws splayed out and kept her from sinking very far. Kellacun hadn't needed to wait very long for the cat to find her once she left the city. Their quarry's known range was actually closer to the grain fields than they were now, but that was the point. She was trying to circle around behind the sow. It was a cunning beast, and had become very weary of the trails coming from the city. But no one came from the wild swamps, for reasons that were becoming all too obvious to her.

Kellacun had spent the rest of the day talking to local hunters trying to get an idea of how to tackle the beast. "Don't" was the advice she received most frequently, followed by, "Settle your affairs." The outpouring of support warmed her heart. It wasn't until she'd learned of a hunter who now relied on a cane to walk, courtesy of the sow, did she find someone to take her seriously. Revenge was a powerful motivator, one she could relate to only too well.

After the death of her parents, visiting her own brand of justice against Duke Dolan had become an all-consuming obsession. Pursuing it had already cost her Joshua's love, her innocence, and as she walked across the putrid swamps of Nalir, it nearly cost her life.

If her attention hadn't been turned inward, she might have noticed that Kaplan had stopped. She might have spotted the chunks of wood that marked the trail suddenly took on a bumpier, one might say scaly texture. But focused as she was, she was wholly unprepared when the 'trail' snapped up and threw her high into the air.

Suddenly very alert and living in-the-moment, Kellacun's head swiveled around, desperately hunting for the ground. She managed twist her body and get her feet under her just as she hit the earth, and immediately wished she hadn't. The soft mud of the bog swallowed her feet up to her mid calves before finally absorbing her momentum. One exploratory tug and she knew she was stuck. Kellacun craned her neck back to see what had tossed her like a doll, and immediately wished she hadn't.

She'd never seen anything like the beast charging towards her. It slithered across the mud like an enormous snake, yet also pushed itself along on four trunk-like legs. Its leathery skin was covered bumps, knobs, and plates of armor. But its most impressive, imposing feature was the enormous maw bearing down on Kellacun's head. In an instant, her entire world was filled with the rows of yellowed, peg teeth, pink tongue, and the smell of rotting meat.

Unable to run, and about to be snapped in half, Kellacun panicked and drew her rapiers. The blades had barely cleared their scabbards when the monster's jaw snapped shut around Kellacun's chest and waist. Her demon-skin armor kept the stout teeth from reaching her insides, but the strength behind the beast's bite was immense. She didn't dare exhale; there was no chance of drawing another breath.

Her head still free, Kellacun peered straight into the protruding, coppery eye of the monster. But her arms were thoroughly pinned, there was no way to fight back against the power of the monster's jaws.

A glint of metal at the edge of her vision drew her attention. It was the tip of one of her rapiers, sticking straight out of the beast's lower jaw. Kellacun's head spun around to the other side and, sure enough, the other blade had erupted from the top. She had drawn them just in time for the monster jaws to clamp down on them like a pin cushion.

Kellacun desperately twisted the handles of the swords, wrenching her wrists while the blades sliced through scales and muscle as bright red blood started to flow over the metal. At first, the beast tightened its grip, trying to end its prey's struggling. The sound of two of her own ribs snapping echoed through Kellacun's skull. She fought against the waves of pain and nausea that threatened to crash over her. Stars flashed across her vision as what little air she'd kept in her lungs grew stale.

Then, with the same suddenness as the attack had begun, the nightmare beast relented and opened its jaws wide. With a violent shake of its mighty head, Kellacun was thrown clear and landed heavily in the mud, flat on her back this time. She pulled in a ragged breath, cut short by the stabbing pain of the broken ribs. Only then did she see Kaplan, harassing the beast from behind, swiping at its tail with her claws and snarling like a hellhound.

Miraculously, Kellacun still held both of her trophy rapiers. With her head still spinning, she sat up and took a knee. Kellacun got to her feet and sprinted as best as she could over the soggy ground. Her breaths were painfully shallow, and with the mud pulling her down with each step, she could only cover a short distance before the stars returned. With a one deep, stabbing breath, she whistled to Kaplan, who saw that her person was safe and broke free of the fight.

Kellacun, Kaplan, and the monster shared a few moments staring at each other, weighing their options. Kellacun realized quickly that she simply didn't have the weapons or strength needed to fell the monster and decided to go around it. For its part, the beast decided that the pointy little two-legged thing didn't have enough meat on it to justify a chase. The scaley behemoth disappeared into the mud from which it came. Kellacun weakly leaned against Kaplan's soft warm fur and fought tears. Is this what her life had become? How could she live up to her bargain with the Nonul?

Kaplan nuzzled Kellacun with her large furry head. Kellacun felt the looming despair fade. She patted her only friend and struggled to tend to her wounds.

* * *

His horse growing tired, Joshua pulled up on the reins and dismounted. The animal's white fur was stained with sweat around the saddle and withers. He'd decided to travel fast and light, forgoing the polished, ceremonial breastplate, gauntlets, and shield that had always accompanied him on his few ventures outside the walls of Central City.

After three full days trekking through the forest and along the river bank, he was now further from home than he'd ever been. Traveling alone and far from home, he would make for an inviting ransom hostage for any enterprising criminals who recognized him. Secondly, his quarry had more than a full week's head start. Despite being injured and on foot, she would cover ground quickly. He would need to use every step of the speed in his father's prized thoroughbred if he was going to catch up.

But finally, and most importantly, if he did catch her, Joshua was gambling that being unarmored would signal that he wasn't there for a fight. After their last encounter, Joshua held no illusions about the outcome were he to fight Kellacun for real. Somehow, with shocking rapidity, his beloved, raven-haired mason's daughter had transformed into a remorseless, and highly capable killer.

And he knew who was responsible for Kellacun's horrid transformation; his own father. Joshua found himself in an impossible position, trapped between loving two monsters bent on annihilating each other. His only hope to save them from mutual destruction was to keep them as far apart as possible. Joshua could no longer say for certain what his feelings for Kellacun were, things had gotten much too complicated. But whatever their love had become, he had to convince her to abandon her quest, even if it meant they would never see each other again.

He untied a water-skin from his tack and popped the cork. The horse-temperature water drained down his throat in a most unrefreshing way, reminding him just how far from the comforts of the palace three days travel had taken him. The sun hung low and orange on the horizon.

The road's stones came to an end just ahead of him, terminating abruptly near a series of piers. An assortment of boats, canoes, and barges were lashed to them, but it seemed that their owners had already turned in for the night. All but one of them. A lone man continued to toil away on the deck of his barge, loading cargo in preparation for departure.

"You there, good man," Joshua called out.

The man stood straight and turned in Joshua's direction, but didn't look at him. "I'm sorry, sir, are you talking to me?"

"Indeed. Have you seen a young woman pass through here." He held a hand up to his chin. "About this tall, with long raven hair?"

The old bargeman chuckled. "No, sir. Can't say I've seen anyone like that."

* * *

Finally comfortable with the distance she and Kaplan had put between them and the… whatever it was, Kellacun peeled the onyx-black armored shirt from her skin. Baring her breasts to an assortment of dragonflies and frogs of the swamp, she probed her rib cage with carful fingers. The fight had left her injured and demoralized. Even free of her armor, she still couldn't draw a full breath.

She gasped a little as her fingers found a tender spot on her side, just out of sight. It was hot and sticky, and when she pulled her hand back it was covered in blood. One of her ribs had cracked and protruded past where she could get a decent look at it. Her healing powers could not get started until it was back in place.

Kellacun muttered a curse and crunched her torso away from the injury. On a silent count of three, she inhaled as deeply as she could, expanding her ribcage out as far as it would go. The stabbing became overwhelming, but she held her breath and shoved the floating piece of rib back into place with a click. Black dots erupted in her vision as red-hot pain washed over her consciousness before darkness greeted her.

Moring approached by the time Kellacun awoke again. She sat up and took an exploratory breath. Much to her relief, the pain had subsided almost entirely. The sun hadn't quite broke over the horizon yet, but with her dark vision, it may as well been the middle of the afternoon.

She took a moment to scan the area for any other nightmarish creatures bent of swallowing her whole, but found only a Kaplan napping contently next to a half-eaten boar carcass.

"Some friend you are," Kellacun kicked the cat on a paw, "wandering off to hunt while I'm lying unconscious in the mud."

Kaplan woke up just long enough to give her an annoyed look, then rested he head on her forearm again. Kellacun then took stock of herself, and realized she was every bit as dirty as one would expect after sleeping half-naked in a swamp. She splashed herself to rinse off the mud caked to her body as best she could, but the water was only marginally less dirty than the mud had been.

With her body still slick, she struggled to pull her demonskin shirt back into place, then strapped her rapiers to her waist. She glanced at her father's sabre lashed to her pack. It was a heavy, unwieldy weapon, better suited for loping off heads from horseback than fighting on foot against a capable opponent. Still, the odds that a wild boar would also be an expert swordsman seemed remote, and the top-heavy blade would be good for slicing through its thick hide.

She tied the sword off around her back and started walking in the direction the village hunters had told her was the sow's domain. Kaplan followed a short while later. They hadn't walked very far before the swamp started to harden up into proper ground again. Here and there, stray crop plants grew wild, their seeds caught on the wind and carried from the fields closer to the coast. Her stomach had been complaining for hours already. She'd come to realize that her rapid healing came at the price of immediate hunger. The wandering crops hadn't yet matured, and she was already out of the hard trail cake she'd nicked from a vendor in town. She regretted not cooking up a piece of Kaplan's evening kill.

The only hunting Kellacun had done in her old life was for fresh tomatoes in the city markets. She didn't know where or how to start looking for a wild pig, even if it did weight half a ton. With no experience to lean on, she concentrated on her senses. She knew what pigs smelled like from farmers bringing their animals to market, so she cleared her nose and let the mingled smells of the swamp fill it.

Hidden among the rotting plants, flowers, mud, and smoke breezing by from Nalir, Kellacun thought she could pick out a trace of swine. It was faint, but definitely present. She sniffed around until the odor became stronger, giving her a bearing to follow. Kaplan trailed behind her, curious about what the funny little creature was going to do next.

The scent trail grew steadily stronger. It was soon joined by a bona fide set of tracks, although they seemed much too small to have come from the monster sow she was meant to kill. Still, hogs travelled in herds, didn't they? It stood to reason that finding one would bring her closer to the sow. With clear tracks to follow, Kellacun broke into a jog, while Kaplan bounded along playfully behind her.

The trail led into a thicket of spiny bushes. Kellacun drew a rapier and slashed a path through them. In a small clearing at the center of the patch, a piglet stared back at her, frozen in terror. It couldn't have been more than twenty pounds, certainly not the gargantuan beast Kellacun was hunting.

The poor thing was actually pretty cute in a muddy, hairy sort of way. But as her stomach reminded her, what the piglet lacked in size, it made up for in deliciousness. It certainly wasn't Kellacun's fault the Gods had conspired against the piglet by making it out of bacon.

She thrust the tip of a rapier at the forlorn creature. It deftly sidestepped the attack and spun around on a hind hoof. Then it tore deeper in the thicket, squealing for all it was worth. Kellacun was about to go after it, but Kaplan knocked her flat on her bottom as the huge feline surged past, completely overcome by the instinct to chase any small, fast-moving objects.

"Don't eat it all!" Kellacun shouted to Kaplan's rapidly retreating tail. She got up and ran down the path Kaplan's body had cleared through the brush. She'd barely gotten her feet up to full speed before running into the cat's immobilized rump. The piglet had stopped squealing, and now stood facing Kellacun and Kaplan with a look that said, *Now you're gonna get it.*

Standing, towering over the piglet was the source of its newfound confidence; the sow. She was as tall as

Kaplan, and twice as wide. Foot-long tusks caked in mud curled up from the hog's lower jaw, while black beady eyes stared back at the intruders. The hunters tales had, for once, understated the size of the foe she faced. It was as big as a horse, and the aura of its stench assaulted Kellacun's nose like an unkempt stable at the height of the summer heat.

Fortunately, the sow's eyes bore straight and deep into Kaplan at the moment, ignoring Kellacun completely. While this was good news for her immediate survival prospects, Kellacun was at a loss to how she was supposed to kill the beast. Kaplan was apparently grappling with the same question, as she crouched low and started to growl deeply. Playing her part of the deadly dance, the sow snorted and started to paw the ground, the needle-like hair on her spine standing straight up.

Kellacun decided quickly that she did not need to be in the middle of whatever furball was about to erupt between the two of them and moved to a better position. There, with sweat beading up on her forehead, she waited to see which of the great animals would make the first move.

As it happened, it was the sow. A wave of muscles and fat shot through her bulk as her hind legs dug into the soft earth and threw her forward like a bullet from a sling. Kaplan answered an eye blink later, and the two behemoths collided in a cloud of dirt, claws, tusks, teeth, and hooves.

The force of the blows from Kaplan's paws would snap all but the stoutest men in twain, while the slashes of the sow's tusks would shred any armor short of fullplate. The raw power and brutality of the fight rattled Kellacun to her core. In the last year, she'd fought for her life at least a dozen times. She'd grown used to the rush of battle, the keened senses, the slowing of time, and the heat of the blood rushing to her muscles. But to see a fight like this, no armor, no weapons but what the Gods had endowed them with… it was unpolluted, unbridled savagery.

Both combatants threw themselves into the fray with no regard for their own safety. The fight was pure offense. Yet neither could seem to land a decisive blow on the other. Kellacun could see her cat was wearing down. The bruises and small lacerations were adding up, and the cat didn't have her rapid healing. Every moment that the fight went on, Kaplan would grow weaker from the accumulated blood-loss.

Kellacun knew she had to change the dynamic of the fight, but she had no idea how. Even if she turned full wererat, the hog was simply too much for her. Just like the monster that had nearly eaten her the day before, she could do no more than annoy the beast.

Her eyes darted to the piglet on the other side of the clearing, watching the fight just as intently as she. Her plan crystalized in a moment. While the sow's focus was still on Kaplan, Kellacun sprinted around behind the bushes and grabbed the piglet. She tucked it under one arm and ran straight back down the way she'd come.

"Kaplan!" she cried, hoping the tiger's bloodlust would lift long enough to realize the game was now afoot. The frenzied scream of the piglet stung her ears like a swarm of wasps. Amazing that such a huge sound could come from such a tiny set of lungs. Kellacun looked back to see that she now had the attention of Kaplan and the sow, both of which charged towards her with a purpose.

Just as she'd hoped, Kaplan was gaining ground just a little faster than the giant hog. She was lighter, and her broad paws gave her better footing over the soft earth. But the sow still moved shockingly fast. Getting caught on open ground was not an option. She felt Kaplan's footfalls approach. Kellacun looked back and grabbed a handful of hair on Kaplan's shoulder, then used her momentum to swing herself up and onto the tiger's back, squealing piglet still securely clamped under her other arm.

Kellacun dug her heels into Kaplan's sides, spurning her onwards down the trail. A thunder of mud-slapping hoofbeats kept pace behind them as the sow continued her pursuit. Kaplan quickly carried them back onto the fetid plains of the swamp. Even with the extra weight of Kellacun and the piglet, Kaplan's paws kept her from sinking very far.

The sow was a different story. Her hooves kept getting caught in the brackish mud. Kellacun managed to slow Kaplan down, deliberately keeping the distance between them and the hog from growing. She needed the sow to keep coming.

The giant hog didn't disappoint. The cries of her panicked piglet kept her surging forward through the muck. The chase continued deeper onto the plain. Kaplan began to pant heavily from the strain. Fortunately, the finish line was in sight.

With the exhausted sow still in tow, Kellacun took the screaming piglet in both hands and hurled it towards a familiar patch of disturbed earth. As she'd hoped, the hog abandoned the chase and headed straight for her offspring, and into Kellacun's trap.

A spray of mud and clumps of grass exploded into the air as a giant, toothy mouth erupted from the swamp. The hog tried to stop, but her enormous girth carried too much momentum and she slid forward on her belly. The monster that had nearly swallowed Kellacun the day before surged forward and snapped its jaws shut, then thrashed its head from side to side with dismembering force.

Kellacun declined to watch. The sow's death was violent, but mercifully short. Sated from its half-ton pork dinner, the swamp monster sank beneath the mud once more. Gingerly, Kellacun approached and fished out a hoof the size of Kellacun's own foot that had snapped free. Shreds of muscle tissue and sinew hung from the morbid trophy.

Kaplan, never one to let meat go to waste, had already finished the piglet by the time Kellacun turned around. She tucked the proof of her kill into her pack, mounted her tiger, and headed back to Nalir.

5
Rat on the Run

The mutilated foot landed heavily on the small table in front of Bladewright, knocking over his whiskey glass and sending a miniature tidal wave of the amber liquid spilling into his lap.

"You're buying me another drink," he said gruffly.

Kellacun matched his tone. "And you're buying me dinner."

The half-orc picked up the shattered leg-bone and sucked out the marrow. Kellacun's stomach churned in protest, but her face betrayed none of her squeamishness.

"So," Bladewright waved the foot in the air, "what's this then?"

"What do you think? Proof I finished the job."

"Where's the rest of it?"

"Unavailable."

Bladewright laughed. "You mean to tell me you tore that whole boar apart by yourself?"

"I may have recruited some help."

"I suppose you ate the whole thing and shit it back out again, too."

"No, hence why you're buying me dinner, then taking me to the King, as agreed."

"Oh, now, slow down tough girl. There is a time and place for everything."

Kellacun slammed her palms down on the table. "I just spent two days trudging through a Gods-forsaken swamp, where I had the pleasure of almost getting killed twice. The time, half-blood, is now, and the place is the palace. Can you get me an audience with the king, or do I have to slice my way through his guards?"

Bladewright's rage at the blood insult she'd leveled sat in near perfect equilibrium with his admiration for her rank audacity. If she realized how close she'd just come to being cleaved in half, it didn't show.

"That was the agreement, wasn't it?" Bladewright said through clenched teeth. "But you're not going looking like that. Go clean up, make yourself presentable. Surely there's still some trace of a lady hidden under all that grime."

Kellacun bristled. "I'm trying to get hired as a scout and assassin, not a harem girl."

The half-orc cackled in laughter. "I doubt you're in any danger of being added to Hector's personal collection. He has *taste* in women. But, there are still appearances to keep up and respect to be given. You want to work for a King? Look the part. Now, off you go, before I decide to become annoyed."

She set her eyes. "Dinner first."

"Whiskey first."

"Done."

* * *

The audience chamber at the heart of Nalir's Castle was a pronouncedly less ostentatious affair than the courtly rooms of Duke Dolan's palace. The stone walls were competently cut, but unadorned. Even here, the floor was tracked with the pervasive dirt and mud from the swamps that seemed to multiply while no one was looking. The entire castle had the feel of a work in progress.

If anything, Kellacun felt a tad overdressed in the lacey, low-cut black affair Bladewright had insisted she wear for the meeting. She had a strong suspicion the dress was more about showing off her assets to the half-orc than it was selling herself to King Hector. No matter, she needed this meeting, and showing off some skin was sure to be the least morally questionable thing she would be doing in Hector's service.

That trail of thought was interrupted when, as one, all of the torches on the walls were snuffed out. Only the dim embers remained, but it was just enough light for Kellacun's eyes to grab hold of. She glanced over her shoulder to Bladewright, who seemed much too relaxed for the circumstances. His calm confirmed Kellacun's first instinct; this was some sort of test. But what kind? The orc's hands remained at his sides and away from the massive battleax hanging from his back. Kellacun wrote him off as a spectator to whatever was happening and turned her attention to the rest of the room.

In the corner of her eye, a patch of black seemed to pull free of the wall and float towards her in undulating waves. She kept her gaze forward, hoping to convince the shadow that it remained undetected. Her swords had remained at the Castle gates, over her strenuous objections, but she was hardly defenseless.

The shadow morphed into a more humanoid form and stood tall. But before it had solidified fully, Kellacun spun around and clamped her hand around its neck. The nails of her fingers extruded painfully into the sharp black claws of her feral form. The tiny hairs on her hand thickened into a mat of black fur, but stopped at her forearm. It hadn't been easy, but Kellacun was slowly learning to master her transformations.

"Impressive," hissed the shadow as it took shape. In a moment, it finished congealing into a man, but not the sort Kellacun expected. He was young, probably only a handful of years older than her, but he was solidly built, with a strong chin and nose.

"King Hector, I assume?" The man nodded and Kellacun released her grip. "Funny, judging by your castle, I wouldn't have expected you to be a fan of theatrics."

"Well, we all have our little hobbies." Hector smirked, then relit all the room's torches with a snap of his fingers. In the restored light, she saw Hector more clearly. He had the tanned complexion and rough hands of a man who spent his time working outside. Odd for a monarch.

Kellacun made note of the observation and pressed on. "So, did I pass?"

"Pass what, my dear?"

"Your little test, of course."

"It was not a test, per se, more of a study in character." Kellacun crossed her arms over her chest. "What did you learn, then?"

"Several things. Mankind's oldest fear is of the dark. You didn't panic when the torches went out. At first I thought you fearless, but now I realize you were never really blind, were you?"

"No."

"Which leads into my next observation. Even though you could see, you didn't look at me as I approached. You wanted me to believe I still held surprise on my side, so you are cunning. Cunning, but impulsive, not a strategic thinker."

Kellacun's eyes narrowed. "How do you figure that?" Hector pointed a finger at her clawed, black hand. "That was a secret worth keeping. Now I know all your strengths and weaknesses. The cat is out of the bag, or should that be the *rat*?"

Kellacun held out the furry appendage and willed it back into human form, taking care not to wince from the discomfort. "Well, your little parlor trick forced my hand, as it were. And few who see me shift live to spread the news."

"Perhaps, but the enemies of Nalir trend towards the formidable."

"You mean your enemies." Bladewright jabbed her in the ribs and Kellacun realized she'd stepped over a line.

Hector's eyes hardened. "Before I took power, these lands were nothing but miles of swamp. Nalir exists because I built it. My enemies are her enemies, there is no difference."

"Sorry," she said demurely.

Hector held her in the intense gaze for a moment longer. "As I said… not a strategic thinker. But no matter, tools don't have to do the thinking."

"So what's the job?"

Hector took a small step back. "I haven't decided to hire you yet."

"Yes you have, your pupils just widened and your heart sped up. You like what you see."

"Maybe I just like the sight of a pretty young lady in a revealing dress."

Kellacun shook her head. "Maybe you do, but horny men have a musky smell I can pick up from down the

street. You're all business, your highness."

Hector smiled approvingly. "Observant, too. Tell you what, I have a small job that needs doing, and the rest of my men are on other assignments."

"Who do you need killed?"

"No one." The king looked thoughtful. "Actually that's not true, but suffice it to say I don't need *you* to kill anyone for the time being. This is a simple scout and snag."

"All right, what do you want me to steal?"

The king tilted his head and smiled. "An army."

Kellacun didn't miss a beat. "Right, then. I'll need a bigger pack."

"Not in this case. How much do you know about Nonuls?"

Too much, she thought. Less than a week earlier, Kellacun had learned more about the tortured souls bound to the iron monsters than she ever cared to.

The experience was what had driven her south in the first place. Had it not been for the sacrifice of one such soul, she would have been trapped inside one of the constructs forever. But she decided to keep that bit of knowledge to herself. She would watch Hector closely to see how much of the danger he decided to share with her.

"Enough not to go looking for them unless I want to be driven into the dirt like a tent stake."

"That won't be a problem, these Nonals are inert."

"Great, but they aren't exactly light. How do you expect me to transport them?"

Hector shook his head. "Not necessary, they can transport themselves. I need only the ring that controls them. You won't even need a new pack."

Kellacun's suspicion grew. "If a ring's all you need, why not get it yourself?"

"Because it's been lost for two centuries." The king moved to sit in a plain but comfortable looking chair.

"Allow me to explain."

"Don't let me stop you."

Hector ignored her needling and continued. "To the east of Nalir lay the elven lands of Vidora. Legend has it that buried beneath the trees of their capital is a long forgotten Nonul army, built to guard the resting place of one of the elves earliest empresses, Vishnala."

"Can't do much guarding if they're inert," Kellacun snipped.

"It was a ceremonial presentation only. It was prophesized that Vishnala would return to her mortal body one day and led her army in a crusade of conquest. I have… other plans for them."

"I'm sure. But that doesn't help me find this tomb, or explain why the elves would just stand by and watch

while I slide in and pinch it."

"To the former, I have recently come to possess information that will help, and to the later, you first need to understand a little about the elven soul. The elves of Vidora have long ago abandoned any pretense of equality with the 'savage races', loosely defined as anyone not blessed with being elven. They believe themselves to be above us, and this has manifested quite literally in the way their society is stratified. The higher an elf's status, the higher they live among the trees. Vishnala's tomb is buried deep within the roots of an ancient Illiander grove. No Vidoran elf would willingly debase themselves by going beneath the ground. It is a punishment reserved for outcasts and criminals."

Kellacun wrinkled her nose. "So the only elves I'm likely to encounter are the criminally insane?"

Hector smiled and held a hand out to the half-orc mercenary. "Oh, Bladewright here assures me your skills are equal to the task of dispatching a few stragglers. Your Al' Kalidian steel is proof enough of that, provided you were truthful about how you came to possess them."

"I'm always truthful," Kellacun snapped defensively.

"Hmm, you'll need to work on that. Honesty is not a virtue in a spy and assassin."

Kellacun grit her teeth, but remained silent.

"So, will you take the assignment?"

Kellacun exaggerated a bow, "Of course, my lord." Hector turned and regarded Bladewright for a moment before looking back at Kellacun slightly annoyed. "You're dismissed."

Kellacun narrowed her eyes and pursed her lips. With a second exaggerated bow, she removed herself from the chamber and closed the door.

After the door had closed behind Hector's newest employee, Bladewright turned to address his boss. "So what do you reckon her chances are?"

Hector shrugged. "No better or worse than the last three."

"They were just naïve adventurers and treasure hunters. I think you underestimate this one."

"We'll know upon her return."

"I do wish you wouldn't throw away these recruits on a mission with such long-shot odds of survival, to say nothing of success."

"Why? You're paid either way."

"It's a waste of resources, for one thing. It just doesn't seem your style."

"High risk, high reward. Besides, the more deniability there is for this castle, the better. Let's not forget that despite my many defenses, if the elven noble houses united against me, I would likely fall."

* * *

It was three weeks into her trek east towards the mountains surrounding Vidora. At first, they had little problem navigating the rocky passes, but as she climbed higher, the passages narrowed. Sometimes there were none at all.

Kellacun struggled to breath. No matter how hard her lungs pumped, it never seemed to be enough. But the view… the view was spectacular. She'd seen mountains before, but only on the horizon. The air this high up was thin and cold, enough that a layer of snow had fallen the night before, another first for her.

Kaplan was not enjoying the expansive vistas as much as Kellacun. In fact, the tiger didn't appear to be enjoying much of anything.

"Quit being such a sour puss, girl. Look how high we are!"

Despite a crippling lack of vocal chords, Kaplan gave Kellacun a look that perfectly reflected the fact that their altitude was the very cause of her poor attitude.

"Fine, just don't say I never take you anywhere."

They pressed forward as the snow from the night before melted under the morning sun. The trees this high up struggled as much as Kellacun. The few that had taken hold were short and scrawny pines that offered little protection from the wind. More importantly, as a dark shadow passed over them, Kellacun realized they also provided no opportunity for concealment.

Her head snapped around to try and spot what had passed over them. It didn't take long. Only a hundred feet above them, a monster glided by silently. Its leathery wings stretched taunt over exaggerated finger bones, catching the wind like sails. Gleaming scales shone like polished armor over a slender form. The broken body of a wild horse hung from its hind legs, clamped in place by massive ivory talons. Kellacun struggle for breath. She was looking at a dragon, the monster of ancient songs.

A single drop of horse blood fell on Kellacun's cheek and ran down her face. It was only then that she realized her body had frozen in place, utterly petrified with terror. With one giant, red eye, the dragon glanced back at the two of them contemptuously. Evidently, it decided that the kill already in its claws was enough for one day and it sailed onwards.

Kellacun's heart threatened to pound its way out of her chest, yet still she couldn't move. It wasn't until Kaplan gave her a not so subtle shove from behind that her muscles again obeyed her command. What was it about Nalir? Was absolutely everything big enough to eat her whole? Kellacun suddenly shared Kaplan's dread of sight-seeing and enthusiasm to get the hell off the mountain.

The top of the ridge was very close. Kellacun watched the dragon shrink into the distance, then climbed onto Kaplan's fury back. The cat dug in her paws a surged forward the moment she had a firm grip. They crested the summit and started their descent from the mountain, picking up speed as they went.

Below them, a carpet of green stretched to the horizon. The forest kingdom of the elves was simply massive. Here and there, Kellacun could make out what looked like circular clearings in the heavy foliage. They seemed too uniform to be natural. However, aside from the suspicious clearings, she could see no evidence that the forests held an entire civilization beneath their leaves.

Kaplan continued her mad dash for the cover of the trees, accompanied by a cascade of pebble and rocks broken loose from their comfortable niches by the tiger's giant paws. The slope leveled out gradually, easing Kellacun's fears of toppling off her panicked mount and rolling forever downhill. By the time they reached the first scraggly saplings, Kaplan had exhausted herself. She paid Kellacun no mind as she collapsed to her side, her ribcage bellowing heavily as she tried to feed screaming muscles.

Kellacun looked back up the mountain and scanned for the dragon. Only a glint of it remained, perched atop one of the higher peaks. Assured they were out of immediate danger, Kellacun turned her eyes to the forest. The treetops were nearly uniform in height, revealing the ground on this side of the mountains to be a broad plateau.

Once Kaplan had caught her breath again, Kellacun helped her up and headed deeper into the forest. The air under the canopy was cool and damp. The sun disappeared quickly as the trees choked out the sunlight, casting the forest floor in perpetual twilight. But it was hardly unexpected; cold, dirty and wet had become Kellacun's base state since her transformation. Besides, if Hector's advice was to be believed, the nearer to the dirt she remained, the further from the elves she would be.

Tree limbs reached out and intertwined like a spider's web, making progress difficult, but Kellacun resisted the urge to slash her way through them. The woods were deathly silent, and the sound of a saber hacking branches would definitely draw unwanted attention to her. At least the imposing density of the forest also meant they wouldn't be facing any supersized hogs, reptiles, or other varieties of monster-kind during their stay.

Kaplan's panic subsided to a more manageable level of anxiety as they moved deeper into the thicket of leaves and crunch of needles underfoot. Unlike Kellacun, she'd called dark forests home since she was a kitten. After a few hours, the cat had recovered enough to go chasing after a wayward stag. The outcome of the chase was never in doubt. Kellacun started a small campfire just long enough to cook her share of the meat before extinguishing it and moving on. The venison would last her for at least a couple of days before spoiling. The pair ate their fill as night fell over the forest of Vidora.

* * *

Joshua was tiring of chasing ghosts. He'd floated dozens of miles down the Dawson River, questioning every barge and boat skipper he encountered along the way. Every last one of them had suffered with leaky memories that could only be plugged with gold.

Even after lightening his load of coin, their information had proven to be little more than rumor and fish-tales. Several sightings of his wayward love had passed through his ears, but they had done nothing but to pull him further away from the home he'd known all his life. Now, he was on the verge of admitting the unthinkable.

Perhaps Kellacun hadn't survived her injuries. Maybe she had finally pushed her luck a step too far and had died alone, deep in the forests outside Central City. His heart sank down to the soles of his boots at the possibility. The thought that the last words he would ever speak to her had been threats made in anger, frankly, terrified him. It was that fear which had driven him this far south.

Now, he was about to admit defeat and begin the journey home. If he found no solid leads in Nalir, he would be on a northbound barge by lunchtime. Joshua dismounted as he approached a sentry gate, then came to a stop a respectful distance away. Only a solitary, ancient, whispy haired man wielding a short spear stood between him and Nalir's capitol.

"Halt," commanded the sentry as he steadied his uneasy legs with the shaft of his spear.

"I've already halted, good sir."

The old man shrugged. "And see you remain halted. What is your business in Nalir?"

"I'm following the path of a young lady. Nearly my own height, long raven black straight hair, eyes blue as the sky."

A spark of life lit the sentry's face. "You fancy this girl, I think."

"Please, sir, has she crossed your path?"

"I have met many people on their journeys, young man, so many that few are memorable. But a beautiful woman riding a giant black tiger? That's not something soon forgotten, even at my age. You are in luck, young man."

6
Forgotten in the Forbidden Forest

Their assignment in Vidora entered its third day, and the forest had proven to be much more than it seemed. Instead of a broad plain, the ground had continued to slope downwards into a deep valley. The treetops soared impossibly high above her head. They were already over five-hundred feet tall, and every few strides forward added another foot to their height.

So little light reached the forest floor that even Kellacun's night-vision was struggling to keep up. When true night did fall, the darkness was almost total, like deep in a cave. She could make out little more than the parallel silhouettes of the tree trunks. In the meager light of the daytime, the trees obscured any clear view of the sun, making navigation almost impossible. She had to rely on subtle trail markings just to be sure they weren't stumbling around in circles.

Except for a momentary sighting of an elf's backside on the second day, she'd seen no sign of the forest's denizens. She was reasonably sure the emerald-caped elf hadn't noticed her, a belief bolstered by the fact she hadn't been killed yet. Not even much in the way of animal life appeared to reach this deep into the forest, aside from the occasional corpse that had fallen from above, and the absurdly large carrion beetles that fed on the unfortunate creatures.

After burning what felt like hours blindly trudging along, Kellacun finally saw something to break up the forest's dark monotony. A diffuse glow highlighted the trees off to her left. For a moment, Kellacun was afraid they had wandered back to the forest's edge, but the trees were as tall as ever, unlike the relative dwarves to be found further up the mountain. This was something different, perhaps one of the circular clearings she'd seen before entering the woods.

As they drew closer, rays of light shone through the trees, pointing the way. She followed them. A few moments later, her guess was confirmed as she and Kaplan stood on the edge of a massive hole in the forest. After three days in the dark, the unfiltered light of the sun hurt her eyes. There were trees inside the clearing, but they were stunted saplings compared to the titans surrounding them. The tallest of them were only three times Kellacun's height. They were spaced too far apart to offer any real cover, so she decided to wait the few hours for nightfall to push further into the clearing.

When the sun had finished the day's labors, Kellacun and Kaplan slipped into the hole in the forest. They moved forward slowly, methodically darting from one small tree to the next. This was the most exposed they had been since crossing the tree line, and Kellacun didn't want their cover blown now.

However, after a short walk, their path was blocked by and enormous curved wall. It ran off in both directions as far as she could see. Kellacun ran a hand over its surface, which was rough and warm. Tree bark. One of the gargantuan trees had fallen on its side. Judging from the curve, several yards of the trunk were buried under the ground, probably from the sheer force of the impact.

Kellacun followed the trunk towards the center of the clearing. Her progress was slowed by rings of shattered branches and rotted wooden platforms. This tree had been a shelter before it fell, or maybe a whole city. Ring after ring of levels passed by every twenty feet or so. There were honeycombed apartments, dining halls, and alters. What little furniture remained had rotted away to mere skeletons of its former elegance. Here and there, tarnished brass fittings stood out from the desiccated wood, but it was obvious these elves had used very little metal. Not a scrap of iron was to be found, but judging by the apparent age of the ruins, any iron may have turned to rusted powder long ago.

As she reached closer to the base of the overturned tree, the ramshackle platforms opened up. Unadorned and without dividing walls, these were not the halls and quarters of the platforms above. Their purpose became apparent when she spotted dozens of flint and bone arrowheads scattered about the forest floor. They were defensive archery platforms. A shiver crept down Kellacun's spine as she contemplated a maelstrom of arrows pouring down from such height onto unwitting attackers. The circular clearings made sense as well. With no cover, they made ideal killing fields for the archers. Apparently, King Hector wasn't the only one worried about invasion.

The small trees surrounding the ruins were evidence of the forest reasserting itself after the elves abandoned the area. At least she hoped it was abandoned. The base was now within sight. Tall, twisted roots shot into the night like the gnarled fingers of an ancient giant. The hair on the back of her neck stood at parade ground attention the closer Kellacun came to the roots. Kaplan must have sensed her anxiety; a low growl erupted from her throat.

Her heart pounded, even if she couldn't pinpoint why. Kellacun could feel the change starting to take hold of her body, but she held it back by sheer force of will. She reached the base. There was no sign of what brought down the great tree, no axe scars marred the trunk. It may have simply grown too tall and too heavy to maintain its grip on the soil. But with the giant roots pulled from the ground, an equally impressive pit remained behind.

The hole was far from empty, however. Peering over from the rim, the surface of the pit seemed to shift and boil. Thousands of tiny points of dim green light stared back at Kellacun. Her imagination assumed they were legions of eyes in the dark, and he stomach lurched. But the truth was revealed a moment later when a small insect landed on her forearm. The eerie green glow came from its thorax, like the harmless lightning bugs she used to catch as a child. This bug, however, sported serrated jaws almost as long as her fingernail, which it immediately put to use trying to carve out a piece of her skin.

"OW!" Kellacun's other hand came crashing down onto the bug, reducing it to a glowing paste. But the damage was done. Smelling the crushed remains of their fallen compatriot, the hive exploded from the pit and engulfed her. Hundreds of vicious jaws ripped and tore at every exposed square inch of flesh. Panicking, Kellacun feverishly slapped and swatted at the assault, but there were too many. Kaplan wasn't sparred from the swarm's anger and roared from behind her.

Kellacun dropped to the ground and rolled back and forth, trying to crush as many of the bugs as possible, but still they came. As her panic grew, the urge to shift overwhelmed her. Maybe the fur would slow them down, she rationalized. It sounded good, so she gave in and let the transformation wash through her bones and tissues. As the thick mat of black fur erupted from her skin, the bugs relented. By the time Kellacun had completed her shift, the swarm retreated as one back into their pit.

Kellacun stood there for a moment, covered in glowing green goo and utterly confused. She glanced over her shoulder to check on her tiger, but Kaplan had run off to escape the swarm. Still trying to work out why the bugs had fled, Kellacun took an experimental step towards the pit. Wherever her foot fell, the insects withdrew in revulsion. She took another step, and they retreated further. They wanted nothing to do with her lycanthrope form. A smirk exposed her chisel-like front teeth. She'd finally found an advantage to being an unnatural freak.

She jumped down into the pit, ignoring the scattering horde. A network of tunnels radiated out in every direction, illuminated by the green glow of the bugs. At first, she thought they were just the result of the massive roots being torn from the ground. One tunnel, however, was a little too round, and a little too neat.

Kellacun stepped closer and ran a clawed hand over the tunnel wall. It was smooth and cool to the touch. Not hewn stone or brick, it looked and felt more like pottery. She licked the surface. It had been hollowed out and lined with clay, which was then fired to strengthen the walls and prevent a cave-in. But it had been built with the stature of elves in mind, not humans, to say nothing of a Casen Tiger.

Kellacun poked her head up to look for Kaplan, but the cat hadn't returned yet. For a moment, she considered going back into the forest to search for her friend, but Kaplan had wandered off many times since they had started traveling together. She'd return when she was ready, and wouldn't be able to follow Kellacun into the tunnel anyway.

She returned to the clay tube and hunched down to fit. It led deeper, veering to the right in a shallow spiral. The glowing bugs kept an eye on her, but maintained a respectful distance. Handy, considering they would be her only source of light so far underground.

She pushed forward, spiraling down deeper and deeper into the earth. The already cool temperature dropped further still. Kellacun tried to count the number of spirals, but her sense of direction was completely shot and she quickly gave up.

After what seemed like walking for a mile or more, the tunnel finally came to a stop at an expertly carved wooden door. The bugs that she'd driven forward disappeared into the walls, leaving her alone in the total dark. But she was prepared. She'd been carrying torches and flints in her pack since leaving Nalir, but hadn't used them out of fear of discovery. So far underground, however, the risk seemed remote.

A few sparks of flint later and she lofted a healthy torch to continue her survey. The round door was deeply carved with a relief of a beautiful elf, adorned in what Kellacun assumed was the height of courtly fashion. A raised ring around the circumference displayed runes. She recognized a handful of them from the inscriptions along the blades of her Al'Kalidian rapiers, but their meaning eluded her.

More importantly, however, was what the door lacked; a knob, handle, hinges, or any other means of opening it. She couldn't even find a keyhole. Kellacun ran her palms over the entire surface, tapping with her claws as she went, trying to tease out any concealed switches or levers. None presented themselves.

Kellacun changed tactics and attacked the masonry surrounding the door with the pommel of her father's sabre. Aside from scuffing the counterweight, it accomplished little. She bit her lip and held her torch to the door, but it wouldn't light.

Flummoxed, she took a step back to consider the door as a whole. It was only then that the obvious problem jumped out at her. This far underground, in a moist, termite-rich environment, the ancient door looked as though the woodworkers had laid down their chisels only the day before.

Something was preserving the door, and Kellacun doubted it wasn't simple varnish. Like most people of common birth, magic was something far beyond her experience. It was much like the Gods themselves; she knew it existed in an abstract, distant way, but had no true understanding of it. She tugged at her demon-skin armor, itself enchanted by magic. Then, her thoughts jumped to the pair of rapiers at her back, and their elven steel.

With nothing else to try, she pulled one from its scabbard and inspected the blade. The metal reflected the light of the torch with a strange iridescence, the runes most of all. Working on a hunch, she gently placed the tip of the sword to the carved figure of the elf.

A snap like twigs breaking came from the door, then it turned on pivots at its top and bottom. The doorway stood open, and a surge of old, stale air blew past Kellacun. It smelled of equal parts mold and rust.

Kellacun stood in the doorway, shaking her head in amusement and disgust. What supremely arrogant creatures the elves must be to key a lock with a simple sword. Who could ever hope to take a sword from one of their warriors?

She could, and had, twice.

Leaving the door behind, Kellacun pushed into the dark chamber beyond. Her torchlight barely reached the far wall. Here too, the walls had been excavated and reinforced with clay. The ceiling was buttressed by a dozen thick timber beams arching up the walls and meeting at the center. Mirrored on the floor were twelve stone paths leading to a glittering sarcophagus sitting atop a marble platform.

But the real action stood in the wedges between the paths. They were carved down maybe ten feet below where Kellacun was standing. Just deep enough to hold their multitude of residents. Filling the entire floor of the cavern, row after row of Nonuls stared blankly, facing their leader in silent vigil, awaiting forever.

Nervous, she reached out a toe and gave the nearest Nonul a little kick to the head.

Nothing.

Somewhat more confident the iron army was indeed inert, Kellacun jumped down, hitting the floor with a crack of tile under her boots. She stood slowly and took measure of the metal monsters surrounding her. At her full height, she barely stood to their waists. They were even larger than the Nonul Petarious had been imprisoned in, yet their construction was cruder. These were not uniform sculptures, but assemblies stitched together with rivets.

These were built by laborers, not craftsmen. The mason's daughter inside her did not approve. But there was one thing these constructs had in common with Petarious; their living eyes. She couldn't look at them, knowing what she did about the souls trapped inside.

Instead, she counted the back row. Twelve Nonuls stood unflinchingly. Then she worked her way towards the sarcophagus at the center of the room, counting rows as she went. Here and there, one of the iron giants had begun to tarnish and rust, which explained the odor. The ceiling must have sprung a few leaks after so long. Twenty rows, shrinking in size until she reached the tip of the wedge, where a single Nonul stood at the head of the column. This one was different from the others; marginally shorter, yet the craftsmanship was far superior. His steal skin was inlaid with intricate filigree of gold, and he lacked the shoddy rivet work of those behind him. If she didn't know better, she would have thought him a Commander of the rest, but that didn't fit with what she knew of Nonuls. Although admittedly, that wasn't much.

Twenty rows from one to twelve. Some rough math gave her a gross of iron soldiers per wedge, multiplied by a dozen wedges. Twelve, times twelve, times twelve. Assuming they all still functioned, there were over seventeen-hundred Nonuls surrounding her, awaiting instructions that hadn't come in centuries.

Kellacun's mind reeled at the implications of the number. Even with all of her unnatural 'gifts', a single monster, smaller than these, had nearly killed her. And it would have, had the soul trapped within it not taken pity on her. Whosoever controlled this army could conquer the world.

And it was her job to deliver that power to a man she hardly knew.

Kellacun spared a thought for the hundreds of souls trapped in purgatory around her. Their suffering these long centuries terrified her. Before meeting Petarious, she had feared death above anything. Now she knew better. Who had these people been? Slaves? Soldiers captured in war? Criminals? There was no way to know the people here, except to slip on the ring that controlled them, which didn't seem prudent.

When she was nearly claimed by Petarious, Kellacun's soul could have been subsumed by the Nonul. Only his selfless decision to reject her soul had saved her from trading places with him inside the monster. Facing hundreds of hungry, desperate, probably insane souls trying to devour the ring-bearer, Kellacun couldn't imagine how she, or anyone, could hope to survive the experience.

Of course before she could worry about that, Kellacun first had to find the ring. As her eyes turned to the crypt above her, she had a pretty strong feeling where that might be. Still in her feral form, Kellacun jumped out of the pit and landed on the cool marble platform at the center of the room. The top of the sarcophagus was carved with the same elf that emblazoned the door. The masons had done themselves proud. The relief looked as though it might open its eyes and sit up at any moment. Then again, considering the other occupants of the room, the possibility could not be completely discarded.

However, the lid itself wasn't seated properly on the rest of the box. It sat slightly askew, as if it had warped. Being solid stone, this seemed unlikely, so Kellacun ran a finger along its length as she walked around the box's perimeter. She turned the corner around to the side facing the back of the room and nearly jumped out of her skin.

Lying in repose, a mummified corpse stared up at her, its jaw hanging open in a permanent scream.

Dry, eyeless sockets pleaded for salvation that never came. Once her heart returned to its proper place in her chest, Kellacun took stock of what happened. The mummy's right hand was crushed between the lid and sarcophagus, pinning him there. Scattered around the body were grave robbing tools; a long-empty oil lantern, an iron pry-bar almost four feet long, a dry canteen, coiled rope, and the cause of the poor fellow's demise, a wooden prop bar snapped in two.

His goal had, quite literally, been in reach when the under-strength prop had shattered, dropping the massive lid on his wrist. The drama had played out long ago, perhaps a century or more, which explained why she hadn't picked up the smell of death the moment she'd entered the chamber.

The body looked male and basically human; an intruder and alien. Just like her. She reached for the prybar, but hesitated. After a moment's reflection, however, she decided that stealing from a dead thief was the least morally-objectionable thing she could be doing at the moment.

The body's trapped wrist left a small crack for the tip of the bar to slip into. Once it had grip, Kellacun wrenched on the end of the bar for all she was worth. She quickly realized that while her lycanthropy granted her immense strength, what it didn't endow her with was additional *mass*. With nothing to push off against, the lever was utter unimpressed with her slim frame and didn't move an inch.

Instead, she squared up against the lid and pushed, but her feet slid back before it budged. Frustrated, she kicked the crypt, and smartly stubbed her toe. Before the rat took over completely, she took a step back and pulled in a deep breath to calm herself. She let her mind turn over the problem, carefully reviewing her resources. The pry-bar was of little use unless she doubled her bodyweight. Her swords were utterly useless, as was her torch.

The coil of rope on the floor piqued her interest. She snatched it up and lashed it around the circumference of the lid. With the rope wrapped around both her wrists, she placed her feet against the crypt and heaved back, dumping all of her strength into the effort. The muscles in her legs and back burned like fire, and for just a moment she felt the lid start to slide. Then, something cracked and the lid fell shut squarely back into place with a thunderclap.

Furious, she stormed around to the back of the lid to see what had happened. The corpse had fallen to the floor, relieved of its right hand. Her efforts had severed it, allowing the lid to close fully once more. She simply didn't have the strength to remove the lid. And most infuriating of all was the fact she was surrounded by hundreds of creatures who did, but the power to control them was most likely locked inside the crypt. With the ring, she could just hand the rope to the closest Nonul and order him to move it. But maybe she didn't have to command them at all.

Kellcaun took the rope and jumped back down into the nearest pit. She slung the rope around the lead Nonul's neck and tied it off, careful to leave just a little slack between him and the lid. Once she was sure the knot was secure, she put her back to the wall and chimney-climbed until her feet rested against the construct's shoulders. Then, she kicked, hard.

The Nonul started to fall backwards, painfully slowly at first, but soon gravity took over and the hulking beast accelerated towards the floor. However, on the way down, it struck the pair of Nonuls behind it. They too rocked backwards, falling onto the row behind them in turn.

Kellacun watched with widening eyes as row after row of frozen soldiers fell to the ground with a painful clanging like hundreds of steel drums. Finally, the wave reached the back row and the roar was over as suddenly as it had begun.

A cloud of dust reached up all the way to the ceiling. Kellacun sheepishly walked up to the now prostrate commander of the wedge and untied her rope.

"Sorry." She lightly patted the Nonul on the shoulder. With her ears still ringing, she hopped back up to the platform. Her lips curled back into a wild smile at what she saw. The lid sat on the floor, broken in two as it fell from the top of the sarcophagus.

"That'll teach you," she said smugly. Kellacun coiled the rope back up as she approached the open

crypt. Before she looked inside, she glanced down at the dead grave-robber and saluted. "Sorry I was late, but thanks
for the tools all the same."

She left one corpse behind and turn her attention to the next. Torch in hand, Kellacun peered over the high side of the crypt. Lying in repose and covered in finely-embroidered silks was the body of an elf. Her face was hidden behind a porcelain death-mask. *So short,* Kellacun thought. Dainty was the best word to describe her, certainly not the stature of a respected warrior. Perhaps the elves valued different attributes.

Kellacun's eyes fell on the dead woman's hands. They looked as though they might just reach out and grab her. The skin was pale, but still supple and unwrinkled. The left hand wore no rings and sat folded over the right. The urge to remove the mask and see if the elf's face had fared as well in death as her hands grew until Kellacun gave in to her morbid curiosity.

Delicately, she pulled the death-mask aside, and gasped. The queen's azure eyes stared up to the ceiling with the same vacant determination of the Nonuls who stood to serve her except the ones Kellacun had just knocked down. The queen looked as though she might blink and sit up at any moment. Even for Kellacun, who had dealt out more than her fair share of death in the last few months, the effect was deeply unsettling. She reached out with a slightly trembling hand and closed the queen's eyelids for the last time.

When the corpse didn't object, Kellacun relaxed once more. She resumed her search for the ring that controlled this army of the damned. The elf's fingers were all bare, which didn't surprise her. Duke Dolan had worn his ring on a necklace, so Kellacun dug through the fine silks around the elf's neck. Sure enough, a chain with silver links as fine as hair lay there. A gentle tug of the necklace and a slim gold ring popped out from beneath the silk dress.

"Gotcha." Kellacun smirked and tucked the ring away into her pack, then jumped down to the floor. Nodding to the skeletonized adventurer, she walked back down the aisle towards the tunnel for the surface. But as she passed by row after row of mute warriors, a kernel of doubt sprouted in her gut and grew until it couldn't be ignored. The elf queen had been clever, and had taken care in her preparations. Yet Kellacun couldn't shake the feeling that the whole endeavor, from the door opening with her swords to the convenient rope and tools, felt too easy. Almost as if it had been staged.

Staged, perhaps, to convince any grave-robbers that their prize was the genuine article.

She stopped and pulled the ring out of her pack, spinning it between her fingers before clutching it in her palm. Kellacun looked over at the wedge of Nonuls she'd inadvertently collapsed.

"Stand up."

The recumbent hulks remained on their backs. Her gut proved itself once more. Furious, she nearly flung the fake ring to the other side of the room, but whatever it may not have been, it was still elf-forged gold. Someone would buy it. She tucked it back into her pack.

Stymied, she returned to the crypt and started ripping apart the burial gowns, exposing every inch of skin as she went, looking for any sign of the artifact, but it never materialized.

Kellacun stood up with balled fists and glared at the elf, but her irritation quickly faded. In her zeal to find the ring, she had stripped the corpse almost completely nude. And although she was fairly sure the long-dead elf didn't mind, it still felt disrespectful. To make amends, Kellacun quickly knelt back down and arranged some of the torn scraps of silk to cover the bits Kellacun wouldn't want ogled were it her body in the sarcophagus.

As she pulled a rag over the elf queen's breasts, however, she noticed a small scar directly over where the heart would be on a human. It was small, very clean, and well healed, as though it had been there many years before the queen's death.

After a moment's trepidation, Kellacun ran a fingertip down the small imperfection that tarnished the body's otherwise pristine skin. It sat parallel to the ribs on either side of the cut, yet Kellacun was sure she could feel something hard just below the surface.

With a black claw, she cut through the skin and dug beneath the surface. The flesh was still supple and moist, but no blood pooled up against the insult. The tip of her claw hooked into something with a *clink*. She pulled it out, bringing with it a ring. Interwoven gold and platinum roots caught the miserly light of the torch with great radiance. The jeweler's work was as delicate as it was magnificent.

More suspicious than ever, Kellacun gripped the ring and repeated her order to the fallen Nonuls. Instead of stillness, her command was answered with action. The ornate commander at the head of the column stood first. Then, the iron giant turned and, looking at his troops, raised his arms. As one, the rest of the wedge of warriors creaked and rumbled to their feet. Their living eyes focused not on Kellacun, but on their commander. He in turn, looked back intently at her.

She looked away from the Nonul's hungry stare, only to realize that eleven other sets of eyes had been cast upon her, one for each of the other commanders. Kellacun could see why. With over seventeen hundred soldiers, there would be no way for one person to organize their tasks. Instead, the elf queen had divided them into a manageable number of regiments, each being guided by the specialized Nonul at the head of the column.

It was truly an army. Perhaps the most formidable ever fielded. And it stood poised to carry out Kellacun's word.

"Put the lid back on the sarcophagus."

The nearest commander spun around and pointed to the row of two troops directly behind him. They groaned to life and crawled up the wall onto the platform. They hoisted the immense pieces of lid and set them back in their proper place with surprising delicacy and reverence. Then they returned to their row without being prompted.

A long, slow sigh escaped of Kellacun's pursed lips as she considered the possibilities. The Nonuls before her represented almost limitless power. With the ring in her hand, she could march them straight out of Vidora and all the way to Duke Dolan's castle. Nothing could prevent her from her goal of crushing Dolan's skull to powder under the heel of one of her iron monsters.

But what price was she willing to pay for her vengeance? She knew too well the purgatory the Nonuls had been trapped in. Whatever the murder of her parents had stripped from her soul, there was still enough compassion left to stop her from enslaving these poor creatures for her own selfish ends. She would deliver the ring to Hector and be done with them.

"Sleep," she said to the lead Nonul. They became still once more, as if they had never moved in the first place. Kellacun tucked the ring into a pocket and made her way back up the spiral tunnel to the surface.

She hadn't gone very far before the glowing termites returned, shadowing her from a safe distance. The blanket of night still covered the sky, so she snuffed out her torch just before reaching the surface. She stepped out into the clearing, hoping Kaplan would be nearby. She took a deep breath of the cool night air, looking for the tiger's scent. She found a trace of it, mingled with another, fouler smell. It stank of stale cinnamon and decay, yet was somehow familiar.

As Kellacun plumed her memory for the answer, something rustled in the foliage behind her. She scarcely had time to grip the handles of her rapiers before the first blow struck her squarely in the back.

Kellacun rolled with the hit, blunting most of the damage, but it still nearly knocked the wind from her lungs. She pivoted mid-roll and stood facing her attacker. Immediately, she recognized the source of the smell; one of the same Hunters she had fought months before in the Blue Dragon Inn. The same Hunters who had been there the night her mother was killed.

And he was not alone. Behind his horned helm, at least three more stood in the dark, ready to join the fray.

Each of them was easily two or three times her weight, but she wasn't worried. Her skills had improved tenfold since she'd last faced a Hunter. Her rapiers jumped from their scabbards as she braced to charge the hunter who had struck her.

An arrow augered into the ground not even a hand's span in front of her boot. The hair on the back of her neck jumped to attention and she froze. She wanted to turn her head to see who had loosed the shot, but she didn't dare take her eyes off the hunters in front of her. Kellacun's confidence evaporated; the situation was quickly slipping out of her control. But, the ring in her pocket would more than swing the balance of power back into her favor.

She slowly returned her rapiers to their homes, making a show of being non-threatening. Then, Kellacun removed her pack and set it on the ground in front of her with one hand, while reaching into the pocket where the ring was hidden with the other.

A voice like honey from behind her broke the silence. "If you are planning on calling up any new ferrous friends, be assured that you will be filled with more arrows than a porcupine has quills long before they can make the journey up the tunnel." The slight but unmistakable sound of many bows being drawn taunt passed through the night air.

Kellacun weighed the threat carefully, and decided it carried the disquieting weight of truth. They had her dead to rights.

"Wouldn't dream of it," she replied to her unseen ambusher.

"Remove your sword belt and throw it to my Hunters." Kellacun complied, still palming the ring. "Now the sabre." She again did as she was told, but on impulse, she popped the ring into her mouth as her hand passed over her face. Praying to Gods she hadn't trusted in years that the magic of the ring would know the difference between being on a finger and in a stomach, she swallowed it down.

"That's a good little rat," taunted the voice. "Now, lay face down with your arms and legs outstretched. And, if it's not too much trouble, revert to your human form."

"You're awfully far down in the mud for an elf with such a pretty voice."

"And you are awfully overconfident, even for a lycanthrope. Now spread."

"The last person to demand that had the privilege of seeing his own entrails."

"I demand nothing of you, grave-robber, except your instant death should you chose not to comply."

Kellacun could feel an unnatural heat inside her stomach, but since she was still firmly in the here and now, it seemed safe to assume the ring wasn't going to activate and suck out her soul. Now all she had to do was play along with her captors until she could recover the ring, call the Nonuls, and escape. Provided her captors didn't summarily execute her right then.

Her best chance for survival was to play the role of defeated, submissive prisoner, so that's what she would do. Kellacun got down on her stomach and spread her arms and legs to the four corners of the compass. Then, overriding her pounding heart and the rage and fear coursing through her veins, she changed back to her human form with great effort.

"Hold her," commanded the unseen elf. The three hunters surrounded her. One of them grabbed her ankles, while the other two put a foot on her wrists. Only then did the rest of the ambush party come out of their hiding places. Even with her head pinned to the dirt, Kellacun counted seven elves, all covered head to toe in mosses, leaves, and twigs woven into loose black garments. They had not let the tension out of their bowstrings, she noted.

A dirty foot appeared in front of her face. It looked small like a woman's foot, but with the elves one could never be sure. Kellacun craned her neck up to get a look at the owner. Even leaning over her from the ground, the elf didn't seem very tall. Her face was covered in streaks of mud, deliberately placed there as camouflage. But even behind the grime, her slender cheeks and bright eyes stood out. She was beautiful, but there was no warmth in her expression.

"Al'Kalidian steel," she pointed at Kellacun's swords on the ground. "You're fortunate we caught you and not them. Only a truly brazen idiot would walk into Vidora taunting the Al'Kalidians so."

The lead elf grabbed up Kellacun's pack and ripped out the drawstrings, then dumped the contents onto the ground. It was obvious she was searching for one item in particular.

"Ah, here we are." The elf leaned down and snapped up the ring that had hung around the Queen's neck, then spun it around in her fingers. "Such beauty." "You should try it on," Kellacun suggested.

She laughed. "So that I can be trapped inside one of the Nonuls, I think not. You must believe me a fool."

"Eh, it was worth a try," Kellacun smirked. She could hardly believe her luck; the elf believed the fake to be the genuine artifact. Her luck was holding for the moment.

The elf knelt down and held the ring right up to Kellacun's face. "I must congratulate you, vandal. In all the time our Empress has slept, no one has managed to lay hands on the prize. But this is where your journey ends. I should tell you, it would have been better for you to fight us and die here. Elven justice for grave robbers is swift and merciless."

"I'll take my chances."

"You already have, and lost." The elf looked to one of the hunters holding her arms. "Bring her… alive."

Kellacun heard a foot being lifted, heard it whistling through the air, but when the kick landed at the base of her skull, the world went black before she felt the blow.

7

The Collar of Perdition

Joshua's patience wore thin. He'd been sitting in King Hector's audience chamber for several hours now. Granted, it was true that his arrival had been unannounced, but it was quickly approaching the time that any further delay could only be construed as an intentional slight against Central city's crown prince, and by extension, Central City herself.

The servants were doing their best to keep him refreshed, but the local wine, if it could be called such, had a character only marginally less earthy than the swamps Nalir had been dredged from. What it lacked in refinement, however, it made up for in alcohol content, which had probably gone a long way towards keeping Joshua's mood from boiling over in the afternoon heat.

Just as he was about to start a more formal protestation to the staff, the far doors of the chamber clicked and began to sweep open, sending the attendants scattering like rats in daylight. A tall, solidly-built man walked into the room with a measured, practiced stride.

His clothing was simple and unadorned, yet finely crafted, much as the rest of the city had been.

Joshua stood and bowed as court protocol demanded, yet the man waved it away and instead extended his hand. His shake was firm, yet controlled, revealing both great strength and restraint in the same moment.

"King DeScoran, I assume?"

"Please, Hector will suffice. Central City is one of my most important trade partners; we can afford a little informality here, beyond prying eyes."

"As you wish, Hector."

"So, what business brings Dolan's son this far south? Looking to establish some routes and contacts of your own?"

"Not exactly. This isn't an official state visit. And since we are beyond prying eyes, I would consider it a personal favor if my presence here was kept as quiet as possible."

Hector nodded. "Done. So, if not business, what brings you here? Nalir isn't exactly on the Grand Tour."

"I'm looking for someone, a woman."

"Ah, you're here chasing love then."

"Why must it be love? Perhaps I mean to kill her."

Hector suppressed a snort. "So you followed her all the way down here, alone? Forgive me, but only love could induce that much hatred in a man."

Joshua decided not to argue the point. "It's… complicated."

"I've yet to meet a woman who wasn't. So, whom are you searching for?"

"A wererat assassin named Kellacun. I've followed her trail all the way down the Dawson to your city's very gate. Now I need only to find her."

Hector's eyes narrowed. "To what end?"

"My own ends," Joshua snapped back a little too briskly. Hector was not amused.

"You are in my city, young prince. Your own ends must first meet with my approval."

"Of course, my lord. Forgive the impropriety. I did not come to bring her harm, but I do need to speak with her. If you could alert your guard to search for her, I can

provide them with a detailed description."

"I'm sure you could," Hector sighed, "But it won't be necessary. I know where your wayward wererat is."

Joshua leaned forward. "Yes? Where is she?"

"Working for me, as it happens. She's out of the country on an assignment at the moment."

"Where? What kind of assignment?"

"I'm afraid that information is too sensitive to share, even with an ally. However, you are welcome to remain here as an honored guest of Nalir until she returns, or…" "Or?" Joshua repeated suspiciously.

"Or it becomes clear she isn't returning. The path of thief and assassin is not without its perils."

"Of course."

* * *

Kellacun felt the floor swaying gently even before she opened her eyes. Her head still throbbed from the blow that had rendered her unconscious, but it was the cool touch of metal around her neck that grabbed her attention. Initially, she guessed it was a slave collar, but a quick inspection found no chains binding her, nor did she feel any hoops for them to attach to. She ignored it for the moment.

The room smelled of old wood and lantern oil. Her cheek was pressed up against a warm, hard wooden plank. Her first guess was a ship, but the air held no scent of salt, only the forest. She tried to sit up, but as soon as she brought herself up on an elbow, her head spun away uncontrollably. The unexpected vertigo brought her back down with a crash.

Instead, she concentrated on opening her eyes. Her lids peeled back slowly as she tried to focus on her surroundings. The room was small, with barely enough length for Kellacun to lie down completely. It was definitely made of wood, but instead of being constructed of planks, it appeared hollowed out of a huge, single piece.

I'm in one of the giant trees, she thought, *that's why it's swaying.* The room was carved very roughly by a crude chisel. The floor had been smoothed somewhat, but from years of wear instead of a deliberate attempt at finishing. It was utterly barren, save for a clay vessel in the corner that was obviously meant as a chamber pot. In place of a door, there was a heavy grate made of tightly interwoven branches that looked as though they had been grown specifically for the purpose.

Well, there was your first mistake. Kellacun smirked wickedly. Her feral form's flat, razor-sharp teeth would make sawdust of the meager door. She sat up experimentally and found much of her vertigo had cleared. Kellacun willed her wererat form to come out.

Nothing could have prepared her for the hell that followed. As soon as the change began, the collar around her neck tightened like a noose. Searing heat radiated from it in all directions, as if someone had poured molten lead directly into her arteries. The pain was awe-inspiring, so intense that her muscles spasmed and seized. Her back arched backward so far it felt like she would fold in half. She couldn't even cry out.

She tried to fight it, to push through and complete her change, unlocking the power she needed to escape. But it was futile. The agony was simply inhuman. So she abandoned the change and shifted back to her pure human form. As soon as she did, the collar relaxed its grip on her neck, and the torment relented. Free of the grips of pain, she vomited what little food had been in her stomach.

Panicked, she ran her fingers through the half digested meat, cake, and bile, looking for the Nonul control ring, but it was not there. She must have been out for some time already. Recovering the ring would have to wait a while longer. Her body shook from the shock. Sweat soaked every inch of her skin, and a quick check of her pants revealed that she'd lost control and urinated on herself. Only then did she realize her demon-skin armor was missing, replaced with crude garments of rough silk.

She didn't have enough energy left to care. Lying flat on her back, Kellacun panted heavily while the shock wore off. She ran her fingers over the collar, spinning it around to inspect its entire circumference. It was completely seamless; there was no latch, no rivets, no clue to how it had gotten over her head, or how she could get it back off again.

"I see you've discovered the purpose of your collar."

The voice startled Kellacun, who sat bolt upright and backed into a corner defensively. Standing on the other side of the grate, Kellacun recognized the small, delicate face of the elf commander that had captured her, now cleansed of the camouflage. The woman shook her head in slow, bemused disbelief.

"Really, your ignorance is almost inspiring, wererat. Did you actually think it would be as simple as chewing your way out? That we wouldn't take precautions against your… gifts?" She tisked, "Such arrogance has

a price. One you will be paying for the rest of your life."

Kellacun tugged at the collar. "What is this demonic thing?"

"Demonic? Quite the opposite. It's lycanthrope who are the demons, an insult to our great Mother Leska and her natural order. That collar keeps you in your proper place. It feeds off the transformative energies of your shift, growing stronger as the change deepens. If you should ever complete the change, it will kill you. So my suggestion, little rodent, is to behave yourself."

We'll see about that, she thought defiantly. "How long have I been in here?"

"Since last night. It's midday now. Your timing was impeccable; it's nearly time for the auctions."

"Auctions?"

"Yes, my dear, the moonly slave auctions. Prepare yourself, word of your exploits has moved by wind and vine. Elves from all over Vidora are on their way to bid for your life. It's hard to say who values owning your scalp more at this point."

"Why am I so popular?"

The elf laughed. "Where to start? The priest caste lays claim on account of your heretical desecration of our Empress's tomb. The Al'Kalidians are quite interested to know who you acquired those rapiers from."

"I don't know *who*, but I'll be happy to show them *how*."

The elf laughed with a confident ease. "Please, don't lose that wonderful bravado. It'll drive the bids into the open sky. You're by far the most interesting lot to come along in years, some think you're going to set a record price."

Kellacun's resilience was beginning to crack. The thought of being sold like a common animal, into the hands of people who despised the very existence of her kind brought on despair. Why couldn't things worked out the way she wanted? She was supposed to happily married by now.

Then, she remembered the ring working its way through her gut. The power it represented was almost limitless. Whatever torments lay ahead of her, they would be short lived, and her captors would pay dearly for each insult.

She concealed a vicious smile and thought, *Believe me, I'll be worth every last piece of copper*. But another, less comforting thought occurred to her.

"Where's Kaplan? What have you done with her?" The elf looked genuinely confused for a moment.

"Kaplan? You had an accomplice?"

"No, not person. My cat, her name is Kaplan."

"Oh, *that* creature. Why something as cunning as a casen tiger would choose a filthy wererat for a companion is a great mystery. She is perfectly safe; we released her back into the forest's embrace. I'm told she followed our party all the way back to this very tree. She paces around its base as I speak. But I'm sure in a few days, after you don't reappear, she will return to the woods."

Kellacun sighed in relief. She had feared the elves might have captured Kaplan, or even killed her for being 'tainted' from her association with a lycanthrope, or some other such nonsense.

For just a moment, the elf's incessant condescension lifted, if only a bit. "I can see this news comforts you. Why?"

"Why? She's my friend. Surely you understand the concept."

"But is she not a simple animal to you? A beast of burden to be abused?"

With the pain of the collar fading, Kellacun's anger was beginning to reassert itself. "I know more than a little about being an animal, *elf*. Take this collar off and I'll show you personally."

"I think not, lycanthrope. Take comfort in your friend's well-being, and rest until the auction starts. By this time tomorrow, you will know precious little of either."

The night was lonely and Kellacun was assaulted by her emotions. She struggled to push down the longing for her mother, her father, for Joshua. The very name seemed to steel her resolve. Her once insatiable love was forming into a hate. He had done this. Had he been honest with her, had he not used her to get to her parents, none of this would have ever happened. Kellacun fell asleep on the bare hard cell floor with fists clenched on thoughts of what if.

She awoke to more elven guards. Unlike the woman who had captured her, these spoke their own language, which was indecipherable to Kellacun. Still, their intentions were clear enough.

Kellacun winced as she was led out into real sunlight for the first time in almost a week. Lashed at the waist and ankles to the prisoner ahead of her, she found herself at the very end of a long line of slaves. Every race Kellacun had encountered was represented somewhere down the line. Humans, dwarves, a lumbering half-orc, even other elves.

But the most imposing of the captives was a great, brown-furred, minotaur. Instead of the tightly braided, thorny vines securing the rest of the slaves, the bovine man was bound with iron shackles and chain. Given how sparsely the elves used metal, the minotaur's strength must have been formidable. Kellacun made note of it.

Only a few hours had passed since the encounter with her captor back in the holding cell, and much to Kellacun's frustration, the Nonul ring had yet to reappear. A sharp jab to her kidneys prodded her forward onto the bidding platform.

The condemned souls were hurried into an unbroken, snaking stack of parallel lines. The auction platform was immense, stretching fully between two of the enormous tree trunks and near enough to the top that harsh beams of sunlight slashed down through the canopy. The bidding auditorium curved up and away from the platform like an inverted clamshell. The crowd of spectators and prospective buyers took their places and the pit filled in quickly. Elves were literally coming out of the woodwork for the auctions; some climbing down from higher levels, others crossing rope and plank foot bridges from deeper in the forest, still others swung in on vines from adjacent trees.

Even to her foreign eyes, they sheer variety of dress, colors, and hairstyles among the collected elves was staggering. Kellacun could only guess at the various roles the different sects filled, except for the Al'Kalidians and their simple silver trimmed black dress. She knew exactly what purpose they served. Set against the rest of their race, the Al'Kalidian dress was so stark and colorless as to stand out all the more.

All the time she sat evaluating the crowd, she couldn't help but realize that it too was evaluating, judging, her.

The scrutiny stiffened her resolve. While some of the slaves broke down begging for freedom, sobbing, or fighting futilely against their restraints, Kellacun straightened her spine and stared daggers at the crowd, daring them to meet her gaze. Most declined the challenge.

A weathered elf, by far the oldest Kellacun had ever seen, shuffled out onto the platform. Draped in silks woven with overlapping spider web patterns and facing the crowd, he raised spindly arms to the sky.

"Elves of Navlashier!" His greeting was met with a surging roar of approval from the gathered masses. He allowed them to revel in their self-gratification for a few moments before dropping his hands. Calm returned.

"Since the first Scrolls, we have been entrusted to the stewardship of the vales and all the creatures therein. It is our duty to maintain the balance and flow of life. It is therefore by divine provenance that we take these wandering souls and right their course.

Whosoever takes responsibility for one of these outsiders also enters a covenant with the forest to put their labors towards the defense and preservation of Vidora and her children.

"Now, let the ancient right of Julkoro begin."

Their voices shook the canopy once more. Kellacun watched with a detached fascination as the bidding process played out. The first lot in the line was a human male, albeit on the scrawny side. Two Al'Kalidian guards moved to the slave. With swift strokes of straight-razors optimized for the purpose, they cut the first captive off from the rest of the line, while leaving the vines binding his ankles intact.

Even though the slave was small, he was still larger that the pair of elves muscling him into position at the front of the platform. But it was obvious from his slouching posture and sunken eyes that there was no fight left in him. The bidding was more formalized than the sort of public auctions she'd seen in Central City. Such affairs there had been frenetic free-for-alls, with bidders climbing onto their chairs to out-shout their competitors, and even the occasional kick to the knees.

Things in the forest started out far more sedately, with each interested party moving to the front of the crowd and placing their bid in the hands of the old elf who had announced the auction. He then read the offers, and announced the winner, but not the amount. Only those who had already entered a bid were allowed to try and beat the first winner, and they were only allowed one blind counter-bid each.

The first human drew only three bidders, and no one fought the initial winning bid. The man's new owner turned her new possession over to the guards to be picked up later, then returned to her seat, ready to bid again.

This process repeated ad infinitum through the rest of the afternoon. Some lots drew more attention than others, based largely on their rarity. Humans were by far the most common, but also the most versatile, so they were sold largely as simple laborers. The first heated auction of the afternoon came when the minotaur was brought forward, and after he'd managed to gore one of the guards in the shoulder deep enough to lift and flip him like a pancake. The poor, completely deserving elven fool flew through the air and right over the side, screaming all the way down until his unscheduled appointment with the forest floor several hundred feet below.

Why they hadn't shaved or capped the minotaur's horns just reinforced Kellacun's opinion of the elves arrogance. But to her surprise, even in light of the guard's death, the auction continued completely unabated. If anything, the bidding for the minotaur was met with even greater enthusiasm.

The cogs of the auction slowly chewed their way through the line of slaves, until only a handful remained ahead of Kellacun. To speed things up, the auctioneer had taken to selling the less interesting slaves in lots of as many as five at a time. Afternoon gave way to twilight as the last of the slaves were sold off.

Then, it was Kellacun's turn. Very few had left before now, while even more had turned up since the auction started. Everyone stood, waiting patiently for the main event. Though she could not understand their melodic language, she was beginning to pick up on a few words here and there.

The auctioneer began his pitch. "As the right of Julkoro draws to a close, the most exciting opportunity is finally upon us!"

With a gesture of his fingers, the surviving guards grabbed Kellacun under her armpits and shoved her towards center stage. They were lightly armored and entirely without weapons, probably to stop desperate prisoners from any last minute theatrics. Not that it had helped their compatriot. Even with her hands bound, she could have crushed the undersized elves with ease, if not for the collar of perdition around her neck, trapping her in this nightmare.

Once she was in position, he continued. "There have been many stories flying down the vines this day about our last guest, many rumors. I am here to tell you that even the wildest of these are true. Before you stands not just an abomination, a lycanthrope, but a heretic, defiler of the forest, and vandal of our beloved Empress's tomb!"

The crowd erupted in the first outburst of emotion since the opening ceremony. To Kellacun's ears, it was a heady mix of anger, disbelief, and anxious excitement. It was turning into a spectacle, and she was the main attraction.

The auctioneer held upturned hands to the crowd. "Because of the… unique nature of this lot, we invite all interested parties to examine it more closely."

Something verging on pandemonium broke loose from the otherwise reserved crowd. A mob of elves pushed, shoved, and ran down the bidding pit towards where Kellacun stood on the platform. She braced herself, but additional guards appeared to hold them back. A mass of elfkind surged, shouted, and reached for Kellacun like she was some sort of noblewoman. Panic started to creep into the pit of her stomach.

Since the night her parents were killed, she'd spent her days sneaking through sewers, sulking through alleys, and hiding deep in the woods. But here, stripped of the armor that had been as close to her as skin, laid bare before a mob of people who despised her, she felt naked, exposed to the entire world.

Over the roar of the mob, a clear, strong voice rose. It was a voice that had grown accustomed to the weight of authority. The rest of the crowd silenced their frenzy and retreated.

At the center of the suddenly empty patch of floor stood an elf dressed in robes as fine as any Kellacun had seen. He stood almost a full head above the crowd. Unlike most of his countrymen, his hair was thick, wavy, and as black as Kellacun's own. A half-elf? She'd never heard of such a creature, but if orcs and men could interbreed, what would prevent elves and men from doing the same?

His ice-blue eyes traced a line down Kellacun's slender frame, stopping to linger in several choice places. He turned and faced the auctioneer. "Why is this animal covered? You wouldn't ask me to buy a horse

without seeing its coat, would you?"

The older elf bowed slightly and clasped his hands. "Of course not, milord. Guards, remove the slave's clothes."

She could not understand their words, but she could understand their intent. Kellacun's knees almost gave out as the guards started to rip at her garment. Her mind flashed back to the night in a dirty inn. The night a thug tried to rape her, the disgusting leer on his face as he surveyed his prize. She had never forgotten that glare, lust mixed with the need to control and overpower. Her gift had saved her from the fate the thug had in mind for her, a gift she couldn't call upon now without courting death.

As the silk of her simple shirt ripped down her cleavage, threatening to expose her breasts to these animals, she decided this was a line she would let no one cross, risk be damned.

Her hands shot up, still bound by a length of thorny vines. Twisting her core, she turned to face the guard on her right. She brought her arms down, breaking his grip on her clothes and trapping his hands between her arms and side. Leaping straight forward, she brought the top of her skull squarely into his jaw, sending the guard sprawling into the crowd below in a cloud of blood and shattered teeth. He would live, but his handsomeness was gone forever.

With one down, Kellacun turned on the second guard, who was yanking desperately on her shirt, trying to pull her off balance. Instead, she pushed against him, toppling both of them to the ground. Kellacun planted a foot and kicked herself up and onto the elf's back, pinning him there. Rage boiling through her veins, she looped the vine between her hands over his head an around his neck. With a quick jerk of her arm, Kellacun dragged the serrated thorns studding the vine across his neck, ripping the blood ways open and sending a fan of crimson into the air.

Kellacun gathered up what was left of her shirt and restored her modesty. Then, she stood, straight and proud, and faced the stunned crowd.

"You came here to buy and sell people like livestock, and dare to treat me as an animal? Well, I have something to say, if you can understand, there is an animal inside me, caged by this prison." She grabbed and shook the collar holding back her inner rat. "But even this cleverness didn't save your guards. Understand this, *noble* people of the *sacred* forest; you aren't bidding on a slave, but your own DEATH SENTENCE!"

Somewhere far below, the unmistakable sound of Kaplan's roar echoed through the trees. Her cat remained by her side. For several long, thumping heartbeats, Kellacun stood there, pinning the entire crowd to the floor with nothing more than her pure, unvarnished fury. Only then did she feel a tap-tap-tap on her bare foot. She looked down and saw blood; her own. The thorns in the vines around her wrists had dug into the flesh when she killed the second guard.

She relaxed the tension trembling through her arms and shoulders, then wiggled the bindings further up her arms. The wounds quickly started to knit. At least her healing was unaffected by the collar. By then, the guards holding the crowd back had regained their composure enough to surround Kellacun. Everyone seemed content to maintain a respectful distance.

The half-elf who had ordered her stripped starred at her still, but gone was the hungry look of a predator surveying prey. In its place was an expression she had seen too many times of late; the dawning knowledge of staring down a monster.

"Er, yes, well," the auctioneer stammered, trying to restart the proceedings. "I think we've all seen more than enough. Now then, who among us wishes to take on the task of this…" He snuck a look at Kellacun's still fuming face. "…human's rehabilitation?"

The first few bidders approached the platform with a bit more trepidation than for the earlier lots, but soon, the gates came down and a flood of hopefuls stepped forward. The auctioneer had such trouble keeping up with them all that little slips of paper started to pile up around the skirts of his robes.

Well, they're certainly resilient little monsters, Kellacun though bitterly. The line to bid on her reached clear across the amphitheater to the next tree. Every last elf in the forest seemed to be queuing up to have a chance to buy her. It was like sheep lining up outside the wolf's den.

Clearly overwhelmed, the auctioneer tapped his staff and called for attention. "Brothers and sisters, it is the right of all to participate in Jolkoro, and may no elf question that. However, in light of the enthusiasm for this human, may I say humbly that bidders of more, *restraint*, might be better served waiting for another specimen."

"How much restraint?" shouted an unknown voice from deep in the crowd. "Give us a number!"

"We do not speak of numbers out loud, brother," answered the auctioneer.

"We also don't get asked not to bid if we can't meet them, so what's it going to be?" A murmur of agreement rippled through the rest of the bidders.

The auctioneer relented. "Very well, judging by the bids I have already received, an elf would have to be willing to bid at least seven thousand gold Kelicks to be in the running."

Kellacun's jaw nearly hit the floor. She had heard the elven word for gold mentioned before, and although she wasn't exactly sure how big a number they were talking, or even what a Kelick was, the crowds' reaction told her they were asking for a small fortune. The assembled elves shared in her disbelief. It was clear that many of them had never even contemplated having that much gold all at once, perhaps even that so much gold even existed. Maybe that was the reason no one talked about price at the slave markets.

Many turned and left in dejection, the polite veneer of equality stripped bare permanently. Still others were more enterprising; groups banded together, presumably to pool their bids and increase their buying power. Quickly, an ecosystem emerged, with groups competing to gobble up individuals and out-muscle other groups. Kellacun couldn't help but feel some small measure of pride at the spectacle.

The auctioneer, on the other hand, found no upside to the chaos. His patience expended, the staff came down once more. "We will close the first round of bidding at the sound of the horn. Any bids not in my hands at that moment will *not* be considered."

The feeding frenzy continued as groups started eating each other. A clear strata started to emerge, breaking along sectarian lines. A small handful of individuals held out to bid by themselves, while the groups tallied up their bids and selected someone to walk the total up to the auctioneer.

He motioned to a guard, who blew a long, low note through a spiraling animal horn. The bidders remained standing by the platform as close to Kellacun as they dared to come, looks of admiration and avarice plastered on their faces. There must have been at least a hundred of them.

The auctioneer rifled through the little slips of paper and parchment, holding onto more of the later than the former. Finally, his review was finished.

"The highest bid of the first round was placed by the Princess Yvonae. Please enter your counter-bids now."

At least two thirds of the bidders threw up their hands and stormed away. They had been tapped out on the opening bid. Many returned to their makeshift groups and faded back into the forest. The few that remained scribbled their final bids and turned them over. The answer came much more quickly.

"And in the final tally, no counter bid managed to unseat Princess Yvonae. Congratulations, Princess, and thank you for taking on this burden. My condolences to the rest of the bidders, and better luck at next moon's Julkoro. Safe travels back to your vales."

The princess showed no sign of emotion. She wore leathers nearly identical to the Al'Kaldians she had faced, except they were blood red. Her cloak, her pants, even her hair was a blood red color.

The staff came down, and Kellacun found herself property of the royal family. Still, the knowledge that her subjugation would be short-lived kept her spirits from total collapse.

Newly minted slaves were turned over to their owners as the guards hurried Kellacun off the platform. Soon, she found herself thrust back into the tiny holding cell she had awoken in only a few hours earlier, the same elf whom had captured her watching over her like a hawk.

"I heard about your little stunt during the auction, rat. You're fortunate they weren't any of my men, or you wouldn't have left that platform alive, no matter what your price was."

"They got what they deserved. And my name is Kellacun. Before I'm done, you will all remember it."

The elf shook her head. "You still don't understand, but no matter. Free yourself from hope; it will only make

your new life more unbearable."

"What's your name, elf?"

The question caught the woman off balance. "Why do you want to know?"

"I'm making a list."

"Ha! Pure bloods don't share their names with nonelves, but for you, I certainly don't fear appearing on any list of *yours*. I am Yvonae, Princess of Valdore and daughter of our Noble King. But you, slave, will call me Master."

8
The Climb to Captivity

The trip to the palace tree took nearly two days of climbing, swinging, and crawling across the canopy. Making the trip all the more dangerous for Kellacun, her wrists were tied to ropes held by one of the princess's three hunters. They weren't there to catch her if she lost her grip. Quite the opposite; it was made very clear that if she were to misbehave, it was the hunter's job to yank her off balance, sending her plunging to the forest floor hundreds of feet below.

Kellacun knew from experience how strong the hunters could be, and knew the threat had real teeth. What she didn't know was just how much punishment her healing power would take. Could she survive the fall or not? She decided it wasn't worth the risk and played along.

She'd faced the hunters in battle three times now, twice successfully. But what she hadn't realized until now was just how relentless they were. Of the six guards accompanying the princess, not one spoke during the entire trip. They never slowed, never tired, never slept, and never, ever removed their helms. By the second day, she knew the truth of them even without confirmation; they were every bit as unnatural as the army Nonuls she'd found.

The mystery of the hunters would have to wait. She hadn't been fed since her capture, and had only been given a few tepid cups of weak tea to keep her going.

Anything they could do to sap the strength and fight from her body. With nothing going through her pipes, the control ring remained outside her grasp. Growing impatient, Kellacun took to sneaking leaves to eat. They were bitter, but she hoped their roughage would speed up the process. Instead, they left her with stabbing pains in her stomach and a flop sweat. It seemed the entire forest conspired against her.

Kellacun grew homesick for the relative safety and comfort of the tunnels below Central City, which, she realized, said a great deal about the turn her life had taken. But here, so far above the ground, traversing tree limbs no thicker than her leg and slick with moss was no time to be distracted by self-pity. She needed to keep her wits about her if she was going to survive long enough to escape. More was at stake than just her life.

Princess Yvonae was proving to have little more in the way of warmth and personality than the hunters that shadowed her. When she did speak, it was only to admonish Kellacun for moving too slowly or too clumsily. The reprimands were accompanied by a lash from a small leather crop that looked crafted for the purpose. Kellacun smiled and kept count.

Nearing the end of the second day, they reached the edge of another giant circular clearing. But unlike the last one, this one had an enormous tree at its center, half again as tall as anything in the surrounding forest. Within its branches, a network of platforms, handrails, walls, and windows enveloped the trunk like a hornet's nest. The bottom most levels were rung with open decks filled with archers at their posts.

At the head of the line, Yvonae grabbed hold of a vine and began her decent to the floor. The hunters followed, pulling Kellacun along before she was ready. Her balance gave way and one of her feet came out from beneath her. With only an eyeblink to react, Kellacun threw her body weight to the side of the branch away from the hunter she was lashed to, then grabbed the ropes binding her wrists with all her strength.

For a bare moment, she fell through the air hundreds of feet above the ground. Weightless. Free. All too quickly, the slack ran out of the ropes. The sudden, painful jerk on her arms nearly dislocated on of her shoulders, but the ropes held. On the other end, the hunter who had caused her to fall in the first place was himself yanked free of the tree trunk. He fell to the other side of the branch, just as Kellacun had hoped. His extra weight pulled her a few feet closer to the branch above before the rope ground to a stop. They swung there, balanced against each other.

Despite the pain in her shoulders, Kellacun pulled herself up by the ropes, then let her arms go slack. With her weight removed from the equation, the hunter slipped another foot. She repeated the process twice more until she grabbed the scaly bark of the tree branch. She was securely anchored before the hunter realized what was going on and tried to counter her movements.

Kellacun swung up her legs and wrapped them around the branch as best she could, sharp bark digging into the soft skin of her inner thighs. She looked straight down at Yvonae gripping a vine below her. "You'd better get that idiot up here quick, princess, before you lose your investment. I can't hold his weight forever."

Completely unfazed, Yvonae leisurely climbed back up the side of the tree and walked down the length of the branch Kellacun hung from. She looked down at her newest purchase with beautiful, cold eyes, and with a single swift stroke, drew a gracefully curved short sword from its scabbard on her shoulder and raised it high. Utterly defenseless, Kellacun closed her eyes against the inevitable.

The strike never came. Instead, she heard the sound of a keen blade passing through rope with ease, and the weight pulling on her wrists disappeared. Kellacun looked down to see the hunter plunging to the ground. But the most disturbing thing of all, he didn't even care enough to scream.

"What are they?" Kellacun asked, visibly shaken.

"Disposable tools, like you." Yvonae pointed to the hunter, who was still accelerating for the forest floor. "That one disappointed me. Consider it your first lesson, slave. Now, get up."

Kellacun crawled around the branch until she was on top of it again, then carefully stood to face the princess. As the muted sound of the hunter hitting the ground finally reach them, Kellacun weighed throwing Yvonae off the branch. Her sword was lowered; she expected Kellacun to be shaken after what had just happened. Surprise was on her side.

Then what? It was this thought that stayed her hands. She'd been captured easily before, even with her armor, weapons, wererat talents, and Kaplan at her side. Now, she had none of these advantages, and she was much deeper in the forest. She still had the ring working its way through her insides, but even once it reappeared, it wouldn't do her any good immediately. For all their strength, Nonuls were slow, lumbering brutes. It would take days for them to move through the thick mat of litter, mud, and roots at ground level. Probably too late to save her from an entire forest of elves hunting for the runaway slave who murdered their princess.

The plan had little to recommend it, so Kellacun obeyed her new owner and started the grueling climb down. It took over an hour for her to reach the bottom. Her arms, shoulders, and feet burned from the exertion. Her body collapsed onto a bed of spongy yellow fungus and she relaxed for the first time in days.

The respite lasted until Yvonae kicked her in the ribs with her hard red leather boots. "Move, slave."

Kellacun was already so exhausted and in so much pain that the assault on her ribs hardly added to her misery. "I can't. I need rest."

Yvonae answered immediately with a lash of her crop across Kellacun's face. "You will do as you're told! Are you so weak you cannot keep up with me?" Kellacun held a raw palm up to the stinging wound on her face. "Beating me isn't going to change the facts," she panted. "You grew up in the trees, I didn't. You've eaten, I haven't. Wererats go through food faster than humans, and we starve more quickly. I didn't say I wouldn't, I said I *can't*."

A ripple of irritation played across the princess's face, but she relented and tossed Kellacun her waterskin. "That's a patch of hubok you're lying on.

It's edible, if a bit tart uncooked. Drink up, eat your fill, then get moving."

Kellacun picked up the skin and pulled off the cork stopper with her raw, gnarled fingers. The drink was cool and sweet, but had a small bite of alcohol. She drank it down greedily, then turned her ravenous appetite on the fungus bed. Tart didn't begin to describe the squishy yellow pulp. She had to stop frequently and wash out the taste with a pull from the wineskin. She ate until her stomach started to protest.

Kellacun felt somewhat better, both physically from the food, and emotionally with the knowledge that her escape plan was now in motion. She stood and handed the wineskin back to Yvonae, then started walking while the surviving hunters took up a position in front and behind her.

The party stopped as soon as they reached the edge of the clearing. The princess pulled a short, wide horn from her pack and put it to her lips. It called out with a low rumble in a complex pattern. An answering call came from the palace tree.

Yvonae faced Kellacun. "Stay on the path and between my hunters. If you stray, the archers will fill you with more arrows than a porcupine has quills."

Kellacun heeded the warning and walked into the open field. What had looked like a segmented sea of green from high above were actually cultivated fields of crops, but none that stood over knee high.

Under the hawkish eyes of the archers, they approached the palace. Everything about the tree's dimensions boggled the senses, made all the worse by the fact it stood alone, allowing the eye to take it in uninterrupted. Gargantuan roots snaked out from the base in all directions, some twice as tall as Kellacun. Stairs had been carved into the roots, which they used to get closer to the base. Eventually, the slope became too steep for the steps, which ended at large, thick mushroom jutting out of the side of the trunk. It appeared to have been grown there to provide a landing of sorts.

The princess mounted the platform first. Lashed to the side of the trunk was a pair of skinny ropes, which ran straight up the tree until they were too narrow to spot. Yvonae tied herself into a sort of seated harness at the end of one of the ropes, then gave it two firm jerks. A moment later, she was hoisted skyward at a dizzying speed.

A not-so-gentle prodding from one of the hunters told Kellacun it was her turn. Reluctantly, she hopped onto the platform and grabbed a harness. Not at all certain she was donning it properly, she tied off the straps around her legs and waist and grabbed the rope.

As she was about to pull it, a familiar scent wafted across her nose. Kellacun looked out to the clearing and scanned for the source. Sitting on her haunches at the forest's edge, Kaplan looked back at her friend. She was too far away for Kellacun to read her face, but her body language looked like a coiled spring ready to pounce.

Even though there was no chance Kaplan could climb the entire tree, no matter how angry she was, Kellacun wasn't sure how the archers would react to a charging casen tiger. She shook her head slowly and made a lowering gesture with her hand. Kaplan seemed to get the message, though expressed her displeasure by kicking up leaves with her back feet.

She turned and sauntered back into the forest, just out of sight.

"That is one smart cat," Kellacun said to no one in particular. She gave the rope two sharp yanks just as the princess had done. The rope jerked her right back. The harness dug into her hips and thighs as it catapulted her high into the air with eye-watering speed. Her ears popped after a few moments, and the rope started to spin. She threw a hand out just in time to keep her head from crashing into the trunk, but the bark chewed painfully at the skin of her already tender palm.

The ascent continued. Kellacun got her feet under her and ran up the trunk to halt her spin. Whatever was pulling at the other end of the rope, she was pretty confident it wasn't a team of elves. She passed the first ring of archery platforms, then another, and another, catching glimpses of the soldiers as the gawked back at her. Kellacun had no particular fear of heights, but as the ground fell away, she felt her stomach drop to her ankles.

Instead, she looked up into the canopy. She rapidly approached a much larger platform than the guard stations below. A hole was cut into the platform, through which the rope was being drawn. From here, it looked like little more than a pinpoint, but it grew as the wind swept past her face. Mercifully, the rope began to slow, easing the harness's bite into her hips and legs. As she grew closer, the hole appeared to iris open, then swallowed her whole.

On the top side of the platform, she spun, suspended in the air and surrounded by an entourage of elven guards cloaked in colorful woven armor.

Javelins rose up to greet her, their serrated bone tips stained with what Kellacun could only assume was poison.

"Hi there. One of you boys want to put down your pointy stick long enough to let me down?" Kellacun spun around enough to find the princess again. She had already been removed from the harness and stood just behind the guards. With an almost imperceptible nod, she gave the order and Kellacun was lowered to the deck.

"Welcome home, slave," Yvonae said. "Now you start earning your bid price. Take her to the slave quarters."

The guards gathered her up and shoved Kellacun towards the trunk. Like the steps carved into the roots below, a ladder had been carved into the bark of the tree. She put a hand in one of the carve-outs and found it had a small lip, just enough for her fingers to get a solid grip.

With venomous spears still eagerly watching her every muscle twitch, she climbed. First one level, then two, then three. It wasn't until her already burning, noodly arms dragged her up another nine levels did the guards signal her to stop.

She collapsed onto the floor and panted like a dog in the desert sun. Sweat poured from her pale skin like she had sprung a leak, and a sharp pain radiated from her guts. The closest guard afforded her no time to rest, striking her with the butt of his spear just below her ribcage and knocking the wind from her lungs.

"You rest when the sun sets. Get up!"

Kellacun gasped a few times, but managed to get up into a crouch and catch her breath. Little black hairs sprung up on her arms and face as the rat within her raged to escape. The collar responded immediately, constricting and inducing pain. Kellacun fought against the change physically, but the rage was another matter. "Touch me again, and you're going over the side."

Either the guard didn't see the signs of transformation playing out across Kellacun's flesh, or didn't care. He brought the butt of the spear up in the air again, poised to strike. Before it came down, however, Kellacun pounced. She grabbed the wooden shaft with both hands and brought a heel down hard on the kneecap of the guard's leading leg, cracking it. He buckled and tried to shift his weight to the other leg, but Kellacun took advantage of his imbalance and spun them both around the shared axis of the spear shaft. She was heavier than the elf's slight frame. After a full rotation, the guard lost his grip on the spear and slid across the floor, arms flailing wildly trying to find a hold, but there were none to be found. He slid right under the hand guard rope and screamed all the way down to the ground.

Kellacun, meanwhile, spun the tip of the spear around just in time to deflect the first counterstrike from the closest guard. Momentum from the desperate thrust carried his spear point into the wooden floor, giving Kellacun the opening she needed to drive her own spear into the guard's face, rendering the poison a superfluous weapon.

The rest of the guards fell into a defensive phalanx, spears poised to strike and cutting off any lines of movement except to follow the first guard on his way to the ground.

Confident her point had been proven, Kellacun yanked her spear out of the twitching guard's eye socket and casually tossed it over the side.

"As you were, boys." She pointed ahead. "Please, lead the way."

* * *

"Where is she?" Joshua tried to put force behind the question, yet keep it from crossing the threshold into a demand.

King Hector, his patience with the young prince wearing thin, folded his hands on his desk. "I've already told you, milord, that I can't tell you that. It is a state secret, something I'm sure you can relate to."

"Then can you at least tell me if you expected her back by now? I've been here almost two weeks. Is she overdue or not?"

"I'm sorry, Prince Joshua, but a clever man could use such a timetable to work out travel distances and a probably location. And you look like a rather bright young man to me.

"Well then can you send one of your other agents to look for her?"

"No, that's quite impossible. Two agents in the woods doubles the chance of discovery," Joshua's brow raised at the mention of 'woods'. "Er, metaphorically speaking, of course."

"Of course." The young prince stood and bowed. "Thank you for your time, milord. I think I've leaned on the hospitality of your castle for quite long enough. I'll be leaving just as soon as I've replenished my provisions and fetched my horse.

"Leaving for home?"

"Yes, in a roundabout way."

"Then I bid you safe journey. Perhaps we can enjoy a meal the next time I'm in Central City."

"Naturally, milord. Good day." Joshua gathered up his cape in one hand and swept out of the room.

Hector returned to his tasks and overlooked the tithe to the church of Rha-Cordon. His priests had done well this month and the gold would help secure the wages for the west dyke. After several hours, a knock at his

chamber roused him. "Come in."

Bladewright opened the door only wide enough to slide through and closed it as quickly as it was opened. "I thought you should know, milord, that our new friend Joshua left through the East gate. He was last reported three miles outside of town and headed for the mountains."

"As expected."

"What does he know, can he expose who sent the rat?"

"Nothing of the plan, I only let slip a direction for him to follow."

"Ain't that just as risky? A perfumed little prince with all those shiny buttons? The elves will have him netted within a day."

"He was driven by passion, he would have figured out where she went even if I hadn't told him. There wasn't really a good way to stop him, short of killing him. This way, he thinks he's outsmarted me."

"And that's good?" The half-orc seemed incredulous.

"Of course. If the elves do take him alive and torture the truth out of him, they'll think me a fool for letting it slip, playing into their natural arrogance. I'll take underestimation over caution any day."

Bladewright shook his head. "Wheels within wheels. Too much thinking for me, I prefer a straight fight, draw swords and let the cards fall where they will."

"That's one method, and it has worked for many men. I just prefer to stack the deck."

9
It Takes Guts

Kellacun's life over the next two weeks fell into a reliable, albeit miserable pattern of neglect, abuse, and exploitation. At first, she refused to do even the smallest tasks, not wanting to give her captors even the slightest satisfaction. In response, they would beat her, savagely, trying to tamp out her intransigence before it spread to the rest of the slaves. But her tolerance for pain was beyond anything they'd seen, and her bruises and broken bones healed in hours, not weeks.

It wasn't long, though, before the Princess herself hit upon the solution to her tormenter's dilemma of how to effectively punish Kellacun; starvation. Her accelerated body required vast amounts of food. More than a day or so and she was doubled over with hunger pains. One of the other slave girls was caught sneaking her food and had swung over the edge of a platform from her feet for a whole day for her charity.

Kellacun quickly discovered the elves were not her only adversaries, however. The palace held many slaves, but their numbers were fewer than they had been recently; a direct result of the unprecedented bid price the Princess had paid for her very own pet wererat. Even though none of them had the courage to say so openly, Kellacun knew many of them resented her for the increased workload her arrival represented.

However, even more troubling than the torments and politics was the fact the Nonul ring had remained steadfastly inside her belly. Every day for two weeks, she'd plied through her own waste in a vain search for her salvation, each time terrified of discovery. A more demoralizing act, she scarcely dared to imagine. Aside from her dutifully trying to learn elven phrases, she noticed that this noble house seemed to show signs of these red colored Al'Kalidian symbols, but it seemed this was some sort of family secret.

Today, she found herself sitting on a plank of wood held in the air by a disconcertingly thin length of vine, scrubbing moss and lichen off the side of the palace. They had rewarded her efforts yesterday with a small boar-hair brush, so she didn't have to scrape it off with just her fingernails.

The horn blew from the very top of the tree, signaling that it was time for the midday meal. Her stomach churned with hunger. Lunch time didn't mean a break from her labors. Kellacun would remain perched on her little board, dangling out in space until sundown. It made the guard's job a lot easier; if she acted up, they just had to snip the rope and wave. Instead, one of the other slave girls lowered a bag of food down to her.

The stiff cakes, dried fruits, and skin of weak beer left much to be desired in flavor, but at least it was plentiful. The elves had never seen an appetite like hers in a human before, and they had somewhat overcompensated with her portions. She squirreled away another handful of fruit in her robe as insurance against the next time they decided to cut off her food supply.

Kellacun filled her belly, calming it. But a now familiar sharp pain came from even deeper in her guts.

The ring, probably caught somewhere in her intestines. If it remained stuck for much longer, she would need to take drastic measures to recover it. Ignoring it for the moment, she resumed her work and scrubbed away diligently until night fell. She'd spend the afternoon and early evening uncomfortably clenched up, afraid to expel anything in case the ring had finally come loose.

Her handlers above reeled her up, signaling the end of her labors for the day. Hunters waited on the deck to escort her back to her 'quarters', which bore an uncanny resemblance to the cell she'd been held in the night she was captured. Her ass was sore to the point of numbness from sitting on the thin plank the entire day. It had taken a few days to get her bearings in the labyrinth of corridors and honeycomb of rooms that made up the palace tree, but now she had at least the lower levels mapped in her mind. She occasionally caught a glance of a red cloaked Al'Kaldian but the site was fleeting at best.

As she walked down one of the main hallways, circles by hunters, she passed by a familiar face working his way up the system of stairs and ladders to the upper levels. It was the tall half-elf from the day she was sold. The man who had tried to have her stripped naked like a piece of livestock before the crowd. He noticed her as well, pausing on the ladder to watch her pass. The smirk of lust hadn't returned to his face, but neither did he display the fear she'd seen in him after her attack on the guards trying to remove her clothes.

The exchange of glances and glares lasted only a few moments, but it left Kellacun feeling unsettled. She was dumped unceremoniously into her quarters, and with the door secured, Kellacun was left to ponder her situation. First, however, there was an urgent matter to attend. Well past the point of any trace of prudishness, she squatted over the clay chamber pot in the corner and relieved herself. Then, with a small stick she'd snuck in yesterday, rooted through the day's waste, hoping to see a telltale glint of gold.

Her search once again proved fruitless, as the continued pain in her gut reinforced. Kellacun threw a cloth over the pot to contain the stench and went to the door. The slave quarters were cramped, to say the least. Across the narrow hallway, Kellacun could see the shaped-vine doors of four other cells. Two of them were empty, their occupants working higher up in the courtly levels. Kellacun was not yet trusted so close to the rest of the royal family, and never would be, if she had anything to say about it. In the room directly across from her slept a dwarf, who had spoken no more than three words to her since her arrival, and two of which were quite rude indeed. The bars of the last cell, however, framed a friendlier face.

Her name was Constance, and she was a natural human of no particular breeding. She had also been the one caught slipping Kellacun food last week while she was being starved for her intransigence. Constance's back still bore the bright red lines from the bite of the ensuing lashing.

"Hello Connie. How's your back?"

"It still hurts, but's it's not so bad. I just have to get used to sleeping on my stomach."

"Right." Kellacun was both amazed at the young girl's resilience, yet saddened by the ease with which she accepted her fate. Captured as a child, she had spent her entire life as a slave among the elves. She didn't even know her own birthday. It had taken a few days to coax the language of her childhood back to the fore, but now they could speak with little trouble.

"Connie, you've been here… a while. Have you ever seen a male elf, about a head taller than the rest of them, black hair, well dressed and really cocky looking?"

The teen shrank back from the door half a step. "Oh, him. You don't want anything to do with him."

"Who is he? Why does he scare you?"

"It's not him, it's his master. She's an old sorceress from the eastern most part of the forest. Even the royal family of this tree fear her powers."

"What's her name?"

"I've never heard, and never asked, but I do know she's from one of the Al'Kalidian red vales, though she isn't an Al'Kalidian warrior in the pure sense. Some of the other elves call her 'The Defiler'. I don't think they'd want her to hear them say it, though."

Kellacun mulled over the information for a moment. Her mission for King Hector had been only a secondary reason for coming to Vidora. The quest that had sent her south in the first place was an oath she'd given to a friend. Find and kill Sinstrinian Al'Kyel. Kellacun knew nothing of the elf, other than she was ancient, skilled in transmutation, and expert in the creation of Nonuls. But seriously, just how many evil elven sorceresses could there be? The half-elf was the first solid lead Kellacun had found. She needed to find a way to follow up on it. But, she'd need to get free of here.

"What is the tall elf? His face looks different than any of the others."

"There's only rumors, but most think he's half human."

"And the other elves are okay with that?"

"No, interbreeding is forbidden. But because he is the Defiler's consort, no one dares question it."

"Does he have a name?"

"Yes, Ulrick."

Kellacun started to form a plan. She thanked Constance for the information, then retrieved the fruit from her robe. Three days earlier, she'd discovered that a previous occupant had carved a rather clever compartment into the wooden slab that served as her… supportive bed. It was deep, and hidden behind a false veneer carved to match the texture of the rest of the wood. With the cover in place, it was virtually seamless. She'd only discovered it while idly tapping her fingernails and hearing the slight drop in pitch.

Whoever had carved it had immense skill.

She stored her fruit in the compartment alongside the rest of her stash of contraband. Once she had the cover back in place, Kellacun sat down on the hard surface of the bed and weighed her options. If the sorceress and the half-elf worked for this Sinstrinian, then it represented the first stroke of luck she'd had since coming to this God's forsaken forest. But trapped here as property of the Princess, she could do nothing with the information.

There were two options available to her now. First, she could try to persuade Yvonae to sell her to Ulrick. He had bid on her after all, but he had also lost, which meant the princess would almost certainly have to sell

Kellacun at a loss. Convincing her to not only give up her newest toy, but to lose money in the process, would require a *lot* of convincing, which would mean weeks of starvation punishments that would leave her depleted by the time she actually reached the sorceress.

With that plan being discarded, that just left her original plan; get the Nonul ring, call up an unstoppable army, emancipate herself upon a cresting wave of death and destruction, then ride it all the way to the sorceress's lair.

There was only one, tiny sticking point with this, and only one way to unstick it. Kellacun took a deep breath and steeled herself against what was coming. She looked at her hand, at her index finger, and called up the change. It had taken her many months to gain a measure of control over her transformation, and it was still far from perfect. As she focused, her fingernail darkened, then stretched and sharpened to a needle-sharp point.

The collar responded, but only in proportion to the amount of change she was going through. Only a minor pain radiated from the collar, which was nothing compared to what she was about to inflict on herself. She pulled up her robe to expose her belly, then pressed the claw against the supple skin. With surprisingly little effort, the tip slid into her flesh as a red bead of blood welled up and ran down her side. For just a moment, Kellacun hesitated as the shock of what she was doing hit her, but she pressed on.

With a swift, determined stroke, Kellacun opened her belly with the ease of slicing silk. Her intestines flew out like a basket of slimy white eels. She hadn't been ready for that, and nausea hit her in a wave, but she couldn't vomit. Mind reeling, she put her hands into the hot, sticky mess of her own guts, hunting for the spot the ring had become caught.

By this time, the dwarf in the opposing cell had finally taken an interest in her, and he started alternately praying and swearing with seasoned impunity. Certain his cries would bring the guards, Kellacun's search grew more frantic. But there was just so much intestine to search. It just went on forever. She hardly believed it had all fit inside her in the first place. Rich, crimson blood flowed freely all over the floor. Kellacun felt little pain, but her head started to swim with wooziness. She was running out of time.

There! A black spot betrayed where the ring had lodged itself. While the color started to wash out of her vision, Kellacun plucked the ring out with the claw. She wiped her hands and the ring clean of blood on her robes, then pried open the secret compartment in her bed and deposited the ring inside. The room looked like it was receding down a tunnel.

There was just enough time left to put the cover back in place and arrange herself on the floor before four hunters stormed into the slave quarters. Kellacun smiled in victory before the darkness over took her.

Kellacun awoke to the soothing sensation of a bucket of cold water being thrown over her nude body.

She tried to reflexively sit upright, but was met instead with a searing pain that surged across her abdomen. She cried out and shot a hand to her belly. It was hot and tender, and a series of small, prickly bristles stuck out from the wound.

"How are we feeling?" Came a voice that sounded like butter cream. Kellacun's eyes snapped open to see

Princess Yvonae standing behind a pair of hunters, one of whom held an empty pail. Off to the side, a slightly built elf in the robes of a priest fiddled with a table overflowing with herbs and small colorful vials.

"Yes," Yvonae cooed, "That's right, you're still alive. You didn't really think I'd make it that easy for you to
escape my employ, did you?"

Kellacun started shouting a curse, but it was cut off by another stabbing pain in her gut. She'd never really paid attention to everything her stomach muscles did before. Apparently, it was a lot. Instead, she laid back and tried to relax.

"I see some of the fight has finally left you. Maybe now you'll be a little more docile."

If you only knew. Kellacun tipped her head up to get a better look at her stomach. The bristles crisscrossing her belly stitched the tear together. A greenish, sticky balm had been rubbed over the wound. "You had your healers work on me, why?"

"Because, I've been charged with your care and rehabilitation. It wouldn't look good to have my newest charge killing herself before a whole moon has past, especially one as expensive as you proved to be. No, slave, your life in the forest is going to be long. Whether it's a healthy and happy life is entirely in your hands."

"My name is Kellacun."

"It *was* Kellacun, the sooner you accept that you've left it behind with the rest of your past life, the sooner you can embrace your present." Yvonae nodded to the hunters, who answered by picking up the litter Kellacun was lying on. She bit her tongue with pain as they walked down the hallway, jostling her without a care.

It was becoming obvious that her self-inflicted injuries were going to take more recovery time than simple cuts, bruises, and breaks. She was going to have to behave herself and lay low for a while before executing her plan. The hallways they walked through were much wider and more ornately carved than the claustrophobic chambers in the slave quarters. In fact, much of it didn't even look carved, but grown. Many of the arches and columns appeared to be living vine, teased into shape by artisan gardeners, then finished by craftsmen woodcarvers.

These were the upper levels of the palace, where she hadn't been trusted. Yvonae had brought her up here to be treated by the royal family's healer in his own facilities. Hardly normal treatment for a suicidal slave. Kellacun began to understand how important, and how dangerous she was to the royal family. Which made the firestorm she was about to ignite all the more satisfying.

They lowered her down unceremoniously through over a dozen levels before reaching the slave quarters again. However, before they deposited Kellacun back in her cell, Yvonae halted the hunters and walked inside. Through the woven wooden bars of her cage, Kellacun watched helplessly as the princess inspected the cell, pacing back and forth, going over each detail with a careful eye.

Yvonae ran her fingers over the bed and down along its side. Kellacun wanted to scream, but she dumped all of her self-control into maintaining a stoic and disinterested exterior. The princess's fingernails

slid right over the cover of the compartment where the
Nonul ring was hidden.

Kellacun's heart felt like it was trying to fight its
way out of her chest. But, Yvonae's finger kept tracing
its way to the foot of the bed, and the moment of
danger passed. The princess finished her inspection
and signaled for Kellacun to be brought in. The hunters
dumped her on the hard bed.

Yvonae loomed over her prostrate slave. "The
healer said you'll need at least a few days bed rest,
even with your unnatural healing powers. Enjoy this
little vacation, because once your body is mended, I'm
going to break your spirit for good."

"You're welcome to try," Kellacun managed in a
whisper.

10
Broken

The forest was vast, cold, and impenetrably dark. Even at the height of what should have been daytime, only the most miserly trickle of light filtered down to the forest floor. Joshua had only entered the Vidora the day before, yet already he was nearly out of torches, and the deadwood around him was much too damp to burn. His mount had flat refused to enter the forest, and in a fit of frustration he'd stabbed it in the flanks with his dagger, never wanting to see the willful creature again.

In hindsight, it had not been his best moment, but there was no point in self-recrimination now. For the last hour, two hours? Time blended in the dark, but for at least that long, Joshua had been hearing small sounds, innocuous at first, but now his mind had started to assign them dark origins. He was sure they were the footfalls of something sinister hunting him from just out of the reach of the torch's amber light.

Any moment, he expected to look behind him and see a pair of huge yellow eyes, or a hungry maw filled with ivory teeth.

He commanded his mind to rest; it was probably nothing more than a curious squirrel or raccoon. Joshua willed himself calm, a state that remained intact for over a minute before an arrow whistled out of the dark and plucked the torch from his hand. It spun awkwardly to the ground and fizzled on the moist ground, then sputtered out entirely.

Joshua drew his sword and pointed it back from where the arrow had been fired. "Who's there?" Fear audibly creeping into his normally commanding voice. "Show yourself!"

The only answer was the rustling of footsteps from several different directions. The prince spun about trying to pinpoint the sounds. Now in the near total darkness, his eyes were basically useless.

"You should be warned; I have been personally trained by Rayhorst Fugalt, the undisputed master swordsman of the North."

Another arrow whistled out of the dark and entered Joshua's forearm, the head passing right through between the bones, slowing to a stop halfway down the length of its shaft. He screamed out in surprise; the pain hadn't even registered fully yet. His sword fell to the ground, and he was completely defenseless.

Joshua clutched his wounded arm and struggled to stop the loss of blood.

Ahead of him in the twilight, a weak outline of a person stepped forward. They were short, and almost certainly elven.

"Ah, so you're smart enough to admit your errors. Unfortunate you could recognize them ahead of time." The voice sounded like an adolescent boy, but among elves, it almost certainly came from an adult male. A small, yet firm hand grabbed Joshua under his chin and tilted his head up to the trees as if to inspect him.

"You're awfully far from home, aren't you handsome?" Joshua nodded, unsure what else to do.

"Who are you?"

Joshua swallowed hard, but managed to keep his voice strong and regal. "I am Joshua, I've traveled far to find the noble elves of Vidora."

"Success! You've found us." The hand fell away.

"Bind him."

* * *

As massive as the palace tree was, even it swayed in the wind. The gentle rocking had made Kellacun sick for the first week of her captivity, but now she had grown used to it. It even helped her fall asleep at night.

Her injuries were healing quickly, but still not nearly as fast as she would have liked. Certain foods upset her intestines badly as well, which limited her already meager diet. She stored the nuts and dried fruits anyway; they would come in handy once she was fit enough to call the army that would free her.

Kellaun finished the cake and wine, then gathered up the leftovers and shoved them into the secret compartment in her bed. It was getting quite full by now; she had to really push the cover back into position.

"They're going to find that eventually, Kelly," Constance said from her cell on the other side of the quarters. "They always find everything."

'Kelly', Kellacun didn't really care for the nickname, but she had started the whole affair by calling the young slave 'Connie', so she held her tongue.

"I plan on being gone long before that happens, Connie."

"Are you going to try to kill yourself again?"

"No, although killing will be involved."

Constance sat on her bed. "Please don't. You can't beat them by yourself, you'll die. And even if that's what you want, they'll punish all of us, not just you."

With effort, Kellacun stood up and leaned on the wooden bars of her cage to get a better look at the young slave. "They won't touch you, Connie. I swear it. By the Gods who have forsaken us, I swear it."

"That's what Frederic said." Her face was listless, like someone focused on something that was no longer there. Kellacun recognized the anguish in that look. It was the same look on her face whenever she thought about her mother and father.

"Who was Frederic?" she asked cautiously.

"He was the last person in your cell. He carved that little hole you hide food in. And when he wasn't protecting me, her was dreaming of only two things; escape and revenge."

"What happened to him," Kellacun asked, even though she suspected she knew the answer.

"They freed him."

"Well that doesn't sound so bad."

"You don't understand. 'Freeing' a slave means releasing us from bondage, usually by pushing us off the highest platform of the tree. When Frederic hit the ground, they didn't even have to bury him. They just threw some dirt over the hole."

Kellacun sat quietly for a moment, watching as a pair of tears made their way down Constance's soft cheeks. Frederic had obviously meant a great deal to the girl, even if he had been a reckless hothead. And while some would say Kellacun shared those qualities, what Frederic hadn't had was an army of seventeen-hundred animated iron statues at his command, although there was no way she would risk telling any more of her plans to the girl. The arrival of the Nonuls needed to be a surprise for everyone.

Some would be less enthusiastic than others.

"It's not going to be like that this time, Constance. I promise."

"I know." There was something about her answer that worried Kellacun. Not the words, but the tone of her voice. It sounded at once resigned, yet determined. She didn't have time to ponder it long before the hunters burst in, Yvonae close behind their ever-helmeted heads.

"What's going on?" Kellacun sat upright with little discomfort. "It's past sunset."

Yvonae pressed her face against the bars and glared at Kellacun. "Bring her out of there."

The hunters opened the cage door and grabbed Kellacun under her armpits, then dragged her into the hall. "Hey, careful!" she protested. "I'm still on bed rest."

"I think you've spent quite enough time in here, slave."

The hunters pinned Kellacun against the far wall and leaned into her. With growing horror, Kellacun watched helplessly as the princess tapped away at the front of her bed with a long fingernail. After a few exploratory taps, her damned elf ears found the hollow and traced the outlines of the cover against the grain of the wood. With a flick, it fell to the floor.

Kellacun remembered Constance's words from only a minute before. Her head snapped over to the girl with a murderous glare. "What did you do?"

"I protected us. You can't win against them, Kelly."

"That doesn't mean you *help them*, you stupid girl!"

"She helped herself," The princess interrupted as she emptied the compartment. "And you as well. Did you really believe you could defeat all of Vidora with what, a pouch full of sundried berries and some thola nuts? You're escape wouldn't have made it as far as the first sentinel ring. The sooner you abandon such fantasies, the sooner you'll be able to find contentment with this… Hello." Yvonae's hand emerged from the compartment, pinching the Nonul ring between her thumb and forefinger. She pranced up to Kellacun with a mocking swagger and shoved the ring in her face.

"What have we here? Looks elven. More loot from our Empress's tomb?"

If Yvonae had recognized the Nonul ring for what it truly was, she would never have asked such a stupid question. One tiny ember of hope remained. She had to think quickly. "No, it's mine. Please don't take it; my fiancé gave it to me. It's our engagement ring."

The Princess laughed derisively. "Wealthy enough to afford such luxury, yet blind enough to give it to such a base creature as you? Your fiancé had poor taste."

Kellacun felt an unexpected surge of fury at the barb. Joshua hadn't given her the ring, but he had chosen her, above an entire court of fawning debutantes. He could have picked any woman in Central City, but he'd chosen her. Even wounded and pinned by three hunters, she nearly torqued free of their grasp.

"Oh, not so injured after all. I knew you were playing up your wounds. Back to work for you. But,…" She turned the ring over in her palm, "…What to do with this little trinket. Perhaps I'll wear it, to remind you of who owns you now."

Kellacun wanted nothing more in that moment than for Yvonae to slip the ring over her finger so she could watch while the condescending little bitch had her soul ripped free of her body and imprisoned inside one of the Nonuls. "Go ahead, try it on," she taunted.

The princess smirked and let her ring finger hover just outside the ring for a few moments, but something in Kellacun's tone stopped her. She dropped her hands and tucked the ring into her robes, completely ignorant of the power she now held. "It's sized for your fat whoreish human fingers. It would slip right back off again."

Yvonae was being needlessly cruel now. The ring was elven, fitted for an elf hand. Kellacun's only chance to wear it might be on her pinky finger, not that she was in a rush to try it on. The ring squirreled away, the princess gathered up all the food and held it up to Kellacun's face.

"Get a good whiff because once the healer says you're recovered, this is as close to food as you'll be getting for quite a while." She strode over to the nearest window and donated it to the crops and scavengers below.

"Now, you will thank Constance for saving you from your own foolishness."

"Not in this life," Kellacun spat the words back.

Yvonae slammed her tiny fist into Kellacun's gut, popping two of her stiches. Her knees went weak, only the hunters pinning her to the wall kept Kellacun from falling flat on her face. Yet she managed not to cry out.

"That your best shot?" She groaned. "I've been hit harder by street kids."

"I can have one of them punch you, if you prefer." Yvonae pointed to the hunters. Kellacun remained silent. "Ah, so we've found an edge to your ego after all. Excellent, now we'll just follow it to the corners and dig the whole thing out. Thank her."

Every bit of Kellacun's soul cried out to fight. She wanted to change, even if it did kill her, if only to have a few seconds to rip the smug little princess to ribbons. The hairs on her arms stood straight up, her teeth started to push out into the chisels of her wild form. The hunters seemed emotionless to her change. But as anger threatened to drag her over the precipice, the image of her mother's slaughtered body flashed before her eyes. As much as she wanted to hurt Yvonae, this was a sideshow. If she died here, her parents would remain unavenged. That wouldn't do.

Kellacun took a deep breath to calm herself. "Thank you, Constance."

"Excellent," said the princess. "We must maintain civility; otherwise we're no better than animals." She turned to leave, but stopped by the door. "In a few days, I'll be leaving for this moon's auction. I expect you to accompany me. Be sure that you are fit enough to travel. I'd hate for you to slip off another branch during the trip."

"Why would I want to come and watch you buy more slaves?"

"There's that phrase again, 'I want.' What you want is of no consequence to anyone."

"Fine, then what possible reason would *you* have to want me come along?"

"Because rumor has it this auction has quite a few humans in it. Your people make good servants, after some training to relieve you of your… wilder tendencies. I'd like a human's eye picking the stock."

"So take Constance; she's a human, and knows all about being a good servant." The venom in Kellacun's voice could have killed an ox on contact.

"Constance has been a wonderful servant, and it broke my heart to have to punish her on your behalf. But she's been here her entire life, she knows little about the world beyond the tree. Now, go rest up, rat."

The hunters bodily picked her up off the floor and threw Kellacun into her cell. The cage shut behind her, and the slaves were alone once more.

After a few deadly quiet minutes, Constance found the nerve to break the silence. "I'm sorry, Kelly, I didn't know about your ring. I only told them about the food."

"You have no idea what you've done, Constance. You've ruined the best chance you'll ever have at freedom, and mine."

"You can't beat them, Kell—"

"Shut up. Just shut up. If you know what's good for you, you'll never speak to me again. I was going to help you, girl. Now, you're on your own."

"How is that different from yesterday?" It was a rhetorical question. Kellacun was about to snap back at her, but it was obvious Constance addressed not her, but the Gods above. Her spirit, if she ever had any, was broken.

Kellacun wondered how much longer hers could last in this purgatory.

* * *

"Yvonae?" The honeyed voice called out from the steps.

The princess sighed and rolled her eyes. "What is it, mother?"

The noblewoman smiled, holding her hand out in front of her in a delicate gesture. "Are you going to pick a suitor this moon? You know your father and I would like to see you married and in a respectable house role."

Yvonae sighed. "Mother, my studies with the vale *are* my betrothed. Like father, I wish to be married to the blade, not to some disgusting power hungry fool."

"But, dear…"

Yvonae walked on, ignoring the voice of her mother as it slipped into the distance of the palace. She smiled as she gazed at the ceremonially Kru'Estaga she had won. Few Al'Kalidians ever won the yearly Duront, and only the greatest of grandmasters ever had a fabled moon blade bind to them. If her parents only knew the ceremonially weapon on the mantle was an actual bound warblade.

* * *

Exactly one month since she had become property, Kellacun found herself at the slave auctions once more. This time, she was merely a spectator, brought along to advise her 'master' on the finer points of picking out the fittest humans to buy. And, she was sure, to let princess Yvonae flaunt her newest, most expensive acquisition.

Upon their arrival at the auction auditorium, Kellacun had been made to change into a lacey, silken dress the color of violet pedals. A seamstress had fitted it for her only the night before they'd left the palace tree, yet it hung over her body like a second skin. She had to admit, it looked striking on her. Her inner girl rather fancied it, in fact. Kellacun might just have to find a way to put the dress on her short list of things to steal in the chaos of her escape.

That had been made all the more difficult when Yvonae had confiscated the Nonul control ring that now hung around the princess's neck, but Kellacun hoped the slave market and the trip back would provide windows of opportunity to reacquire it. But first she would need a suitable duplicate to replace it with. That part, at least, wouldn't be as difficult as she'd first feared.

The purple dress and ever-present ring of guards surrounding Kellacun had succeeded in drawing plenty of attention to her, no doubt as Yvonae had hoped. The princess paraded about in the Al'Kalidian red leathers and brilliant flowing Cadacka. Kellacun thought she noticed as many disapproving glares as much as those of aw. What Yvonae probably hadn't anticipated was the kind of attention Kellacun was bringing. The young elves looked up to Kellacun with the sort of mixture of adoration and terror that a child might give a lion. Some of the braver boys snuck past the hunters to lay a hand on her leg, just to run away screaming and giggling at their friends.

The adults, meanwhile, we less enthusiastic. Kellacun's ears were almost too sensitive for such a large crowd, but even over the flood of background noise, she could pick out fragments of the sorts of rumors swirling around her. She was surprised that she could understand what the elves were saying. Their foreign honeyed tongue seemed as common as her own.

Yvonae smiled as they moved through the crowd. She leaned in with a whisper. "I can guess by the stark confusion on your face, the collar is beginning to claim you. As your will is broken, its powers will manifest. You and I will be linked more and more until your will is completely mine."

Kellacun fought the terror inside of her. What did that mean? Would the elf be able to read her mind? Was she going to become like the hunters? Her thoughts were soon overcome by the whispers she could pick up from the on looking crowd.

"Seven thousand kelicks, can you imagine?"

"Seven thousand was just the floor, who knows what the spoiled brat paid in the end."

"You could buy enough slaves to run an entire tree for that much gold."

"I bet she bought those leathers too. No elf had ever won a Duront at such a young age."

"I heard the rat can't even work. She's too wild."

"She's killed six guards already."

"I heard it was a dozen."

"For what, a pet? Is Yvonae even *trying* to rehabilitate her?"

What really struck Kellacun was how open with their criticism and condemnation the crowd was being, right in front of Yvonae's hunters. Kellacun was beginning to think the princess had badly miscalculated her people's reaction. Her extravagance was sowing disunity. The populace grew restless. Was this why the princess wanted her? Out of vanity or necessity?

Kellacun decided driving the dagger in deeper could be handy in the future. But how best to do it? Drive up their fear of her savagery, or try and garner sympathy?

She'd have to give it more reflection. In the meantime, she simply smiled at and teased the children.

On the platform above, the far doors opened and twin columns of captives were led onto the deck. There were indeed a large share of humans in today's queue, enough that the handful of dwarves stood out for standing low. But immediately apparent, even to Kellacun, was the reappearance of a certain minotaur in the lineup. Apparently, he had proven to be more than his buyer could handle.

Kellacun made a note to try and introduce herself.

The same ancient elf who had presided over Kellacun's auction, and from all appearances every other auction for the last thousand years, stepped up to the auctioneer's podium. He recited the now-familiar introduction...

"Elves of Navlashier. Since the first scrolls, we have been entrusted to the stewardship of these woods and all the creatures therein—" and the rite was underway. The crowd today was noticeably smaller than the one Kellacun stood before the day she was auctioned, and many of those who had shown up were clustered around the sideshow that she had become.

Yvonae, seemingly oblivious to the growing hostility of the crowd, stepped next to Kellacun and leaned in to speak privately. "Point out only the strongest, healthiest looking slaves. You were expensive; we need to resupply the palace's laborers."

"Don't worry, princess, I'll get you the strongest available." *And recruit myself a small army in the process.* She suppressed a smirk as the first slave was paraded in front of the bidders. He was a human, but slim, almost gaunt. His face looked listless, his eyes flat. He would be of little use to either Yvonae *or* Kellacun.

The man was purchased with little fan fair and the cycle repeated, and repeated. Kellacun made occasional recommendations, of which Yvonae bid on three, winning all of them. Guilt crept into Kellacun's heart. She was collaborating with the enemy to buy and sell souls, but she saw no alternative. Her escape plan had become more complicated, and she couldn't afford to rock the boat. Besides, if the princess didn't buy them, they would go to some other tree, or back into the stockades like cattle. Kellacun hadn't captured them, hadn't placed them on the block, and wasn't putting up the gold to purchase them.

The main event came to the stage as over a dozen guards dragged the minotaur to the stage. His arms, ankles, waist, and neck were bound by thick leather straps attached to chains held by the guards. Apparently, they'd learned their lesson the last time the brute had been put up and gored a guard to death. The chains represented more metal than Kellacun had seen in one place since she'd entered the forest.

"What about him?" She lobbied the princess.

"The bullman? Are you crazy?"

"Think about it, he's stronger than any six humans combined. You said the palace needed laborers."

"Yes, but not mindless killers."

"Some have said wererats are mindless killers, yet you bought me. Look at him, he's magnificent." Kellacun watched intently as Yvonae's eyes took in the beast. Her face was awash with avarice, bordering on lust the power the spectacle would bring. But the trance broke and she shook her head. "No, your beast is constrained by your collar. He is a beast at all times, with no way to control it. Let some other fool try their luck."

Damn. Kellacun had really hoped she would take the bait. At the right moment, a rampaging beast could have been exactly what she needed. The rest of the auction ground toward its conclusion. Only a few lots remained, of which there were only three humans. A young woman no older than Kellacun herself, a man graying at the temples, and another, younger male. He wore the same simple garment as the rest, his hair was wild and face dirty, but he was fit and stood tall. There was something regal about him. Kellacun leaned closer to try and get a better look. The startled gasp escaped her lips before she could stop it. It was Joshua standing on the stage, there could be no doubt. Yvonae turned her head at the sound of Kellacun's surprise. She tried to hide it, but she could feel her cheeks turning red and hot with blood. What was he doing here? Had he come after her? It seemed impossible; he'd never been more than five miles outside the walls of Central City in all his life. Why would he travel hundreds of miles, only to be captured? It wasn't an organized kidnapping; they weren't holding him for ransom. They probably didn't even know who stood before them.

Before Kellacun had the chance to absorb and process what she was seeing, the bidding started. "Bid on him," she commanded Yvonae.

The princess merely laughed. "You are here to advise, not make the calls."

"Look at him. He's young and in excellent shape."

"He's fit, yes, but for bedding young women, not doing work. We're here to rebuild our labor force, not buy you a treat. Besides, he is missing his right hand. Better suited for kitchen work than hard labor."

The first round of bidders stepped forward and handed their slips to the weathered auctioneer. Among them was a familiar face; the half-elf Ulrick. Kellacun hovered on the verge of panic. She didn't know what motivations had propelled him so far south and into the clutches of the elves. Was he here to rescue her, or to extract revenge for her attempt to murder his father?

Without interrogating him, there was no way for her to know with certainty, and the thought of him being sold to the Defiler sent frost through her nerves. The scene awakened emotions in Kellacun's heart that she had though dead for months. Perhaps they had merely been dormant.

"Royal blood runs through his veins. He's a very rare catch."

"A puffed-up peacock, then. Even more useless as a slave."

The auctioneer interrupted the argument. "The highest bid of the first round goes to Ulrick, submitted on behalf of her Lady Sinstrinian. Please ready your counter bids now."

Kellacun turned to Yvonae, pleading in her eyes. For the first time, she wanted something from the elf, and she was willing to bargain to get it. The change in her attitude didn't go unnoticed by the princess.

"Why do you care about this man? What is he to you?"

Kellacun looked at her feet, but remained silent. A burst of insight raced across Yvonae's delicate face. "He's your fiancé."

Unexpected tears erupted from Kellacun's eyes. She had no control over them. She expected the princess to cackle, to crow another victory of cruelty. But instead, she put her hand on Kellacun's arm. "Is her your mate or not?"

"Yes. At least he was, once."

"Why is he here?"

"I don't know."

Bidders were starting to return to the platform with their final offers.

"There's not much time. If I bid on him, what do I get in return?"

So, there it was. Kellacun was being given the chance to bargain for her lover's life, even though she had no way to know his intentions now. But what did she have to offer? She had been stripped of everything she owned. Everything she had fought for. She had nothing left to give, except...

"My obedience."

Yvonae nodded curtly. "So, let us be clear. If I agree to buy your mate, you agree to embrace your role as servant, to abandon your plots and schemes. To accept your new life?"

Kellacun straightened her back, and lifted her head to its full height. "Yes," she whispered solemnly.

"Done." Hurriedly, Yvonae tore a strip of parchment and scribbled a bid onto it. She then ran forward and pressed the slip into the auctioneer's waiting hand. They argued quietly for a few moments, probably because the rules of the right didn't actually allow her to place a counter-bid, since she hadn't been one of the original bidders. In the end, however, Yvonae's charms and influence won him over. The breach of protocol did not sit well with the already riled audience.

If Yvonae heard their discontent, she showed no outward signs of it as she walked back to stand in front of Kellacun.

The auctioneer finished reviewing the second round of bidding, and made his fateful announcement. "The high bidder was our beloved princess Yvonae. That concludes this Moon's rite of Julkoro. Safe journeys to all."

The auction over, a triumphant princess turned to face her prized possession. "There, I've done as you requested. Now, it's time to hold up your end of the agreement. What is your name?"

Kellacun's stomach boiled as she glared at the elf, but all other trails were now blocked. With a force of will, she swallowed her pride and answered her Master. "Slave."

Yvonae smiled broadly, a magnificent sight.

"Excellent. Now, get on your knees and kiss my foot." The collar choked down on her throat, almost as if it could anticipate the outburst of violence bubbling right under

Kellacun's skin. Seething with anger, resentment, and helplessness, Kellacun forced her inner rat back into compliance and stooped down on one knee. Bile rising in her throat, she knelt her face down to the ground, and placed her lips on the mud of Yvonae's boot. Kellacun would risk her own life with her plots, but if Joshua did indeed come to find her, he still loved her. The last remnant of her past was in her hands. She couldn't willfully destroy it. "I will always obey, my master."

The adventure continues in

The Wererat's Tale
Book IV: Tiers of Valdore